My Turn

Sue,

Thank you for helping me get the story right.

Leslie Mire

What readers are saying about the continuing saga of the Nash Sisters

This second novel about the Nash sisters doesn't disappoint. Set in North Carolina at the end of WW II, it continues the story of three strong women and their families as they support each other in times of trouble. The dropping of the atom bomb, Jim Crow laws, and mental illness are among the challenges they face and overcome. This is an engaging story told in part through the round-robin letters the sisters write to each other. It reaches the heart of what it means to be a loving family.

Canadian Amazon Customer

Heartwarming story about a Southern family. This is a story about a family who love and support each other through life's joys and sorrows, with a good dose of humor thrown in. I felt like the world was a little brighter place after I read it. Love the Nash sisters!

Phyllis Foster

Captivating fast-moving novel. I picked this book up at a coffee shop in Surf City, North Carolina, on a whim. On my way to work, I stopped by the beach to dive in a few minutes before my shift started.... I couldn't wait to get home and be whisked away. I just finished the book the same day and look forward to returning to the coffee shop for the next book! I absolutely recommend it. The author writes in such a way that you are transported to a different place totally engaged in the storylines of the characters.

Gilchrist Mustin

My Turn

Leatha Marie

Printed in the United States of America
ISBN 978-1-956543-15-5

Book Design by CSinclaire Write-Design
Cover Design by Csinclaire Write-Design
Cover Art by Bob Ritchie

WRITEWAY
PUBLISHING

Books by Leatha Marie

The Nash Sisters (Book 1)

A heart-warming novel introducing four sisters
growing up in the rural South in the
1920s, 1930s, and 1940s

Happiness Doesn't Come Easily (Book 2)

Life brings hardship, joy, and new beginnings
to the Nash Sisters, and through it all,
family love and support are always there.

For Susan Hoyt Bloom, whom we lost this year.
She was my friend, traveling companion, and
colleague for more than thirty years.
She encouraged me all along the way
to get these stories written.
I have to figure out how
to send this one to heaven.
She needs to read it.

My Turn

THE NASH FAMILY IS growing. Every member is uniquely important to the story. The sisters want to tell you about friends and relations who have impacted their lives.

In the Nash sisters novels, each character tells the stories from their point of view. To keep it all straight, notice who's speaking by the character name at the beginning of each chapter. Before you start reading, each one wants to tell you about who they are. If you have read the earlier Nash sisters books, you'll be sure to recognize all the sisters!

Enjoy,
Leatha Marie

Ethel

I am the oldest and most experienced in the ways of the world. Dianne, my older sister, left me in charge by dying of the BIG C way too young. She'd already lost her husband Joe. He was the best married-a-Nash-sister man for Dianne and their little girl, Suzy. Suzy was only ten when her mother died. Saddest thing in the world for a child to lose both parents.

I need to tell you about the men in my life. Frank was my first love, but he was tangled up in a family that did not want him to have a child out of wedlock.

Well, there wasn't much they could do about that. Our baby Marie was born without their permission. I don't think Frank's goals in life included marriage to me over his parents demands. So, mine didn't involve marriage to him either. Marie and I live a good life, with Frank on the outside. Then there was Larry. I met him when Marie was a baby. He was a nice enough guy, but traveled too much. During the Depression he didn't come back from a trip. I think because he knew I didn't like the idea of marriage. Then I met George. He was the best man I knew, so I married him. He treated Marie like his own and was so good to me when my sister died. George was the one who came up with the idea of officially adopting Suzy. He schemed with Dianne just before she died. Marie's best friend and cousin became her sister. Then dang it all, George died. I was lonesome and trying to build a business a long way from my sisters. One day in 1945, Larry came back. He missed me and I missed him. My sister Annie told me I better marry him or he would go away again. Larry wanted it too, so I did marry him.

Besides Larry, Marie and Suzy are central to me being a good human being. Marie got married to Al. She tried to do it secretly, but Suzy wouldn't let her. Suzy invited us all to the house to say congratulations. It surprised Marie, especially because Frank showed up. She and Al have three children now and one more on the way. She's a good momma. More patient than me and a lot smarter. She was going to NC State College, but marriage and babies made her halt that. Suzy is the businesswoman in the family. Like me, she likes making things happen and finding ways to make money. When I need to be elsewhere, Larry and Suzy run The Kooler and Washerette. Those two together are better than me at making a profit. Suzy is working on commercial success. Sometime soon I hope she makes room for a family.

Annie

I am the middle child now. There is science about what happens to middle children. We are the peacemakers. Middle children are sometimes hidden. I believe you have to put out a shining light or nobody notices you. Ethel calls me the prissy one. I just like to have fun and look good when I do. After the crash of '29, I moved to Washington, DC, to get a job. I knew a job in our nation's capital would pay better than living off our parents' farm. I found a job on the first trip and got a room in a boarding house for women. After dating several men, I found a good man and the love of my life. It happened when I took a new job in the War Department. He was my boss. Jonathan Walsh was a widower with a baby. His wife died while giving birth. I had an instant family of my own when we married.

Jon's job affords us a nice house, car, and anything I need. Actually, anything I want. He spoils me. I was able to pay the bills when my Nash family needed to travel to North Carolina and help our sister, Caroline. There has been happiness and tragedy in our Nash family. Ethel is the sturdy foundation of our family.

Jon and I give financial assistance. It makes Ethel mad. She says it's Daddy Warbucks showing off.

Jon brought Lisa to the marriage, and we had three more children. Unfortunately, we lost one in a difficult childbirth. It was horrendous. The baby was named Thomas. Baby Thomas is now in heaven with my sister, momma, and daddy. I know they are holding each other.

I can't stop talking before I tell you about Lelia. She is the beautiful black woman in our life. She faces a lot in a racist society. I stand up for and with her through it. And Lelia holds me and our family together through good times and bad.

Caroline

I am the youngest of the Nash sisters. When you look at my life you will agree that I am the most pitiful here. I haven't made the best choices, but it is not entirely my fault. I am mentally ill. Have been most, if not all, of my life. I burned down a barn and someone was in it. I have been in jail. I held two children down in a basement because I thought Japan was close by and the US was bombing them. I have been held in custody much of my life at the insane asylum in Raleigh. I thank God for my sisters, because every time I blew apart the pieces of me, they were there to pick them up. Most of all I am thankful for the insane asylum, now more respectably called Dorothea Dix Hill. Dr. Redmond, the best psych doctor in the world, works to get me well. The nurses through the years test and take notes. We have to have a report card, you know. I am most grateful for Belle Porter. She is called a house mother, but she is much more to me. Belle, a large black woman with the warmest smile, is like my momma. She has faith in my recovery, always, like my own momma did. You know how kind and supportive she is because she recommended that I become a nanny for her grandchildren. Then I held them in the basement against their will because I got scared. Belle forgave me. Who else but a mother does that? Maybe sisters do too.

Over the years I have learned a lot about mental illness therapy, treatment, medicine, and healing. I discovered how to allow anxiety, anger, and sadness so I can see it. That way I get help when it is bigger than I can manage alone. I now understand what normal looks like for me. I can accept myself and love me. My secret weapon, besides the medication, is using humor to lighten things up. I know being well daily is not realistic, but becoming better over months and years fits my plan.

One more cool thing you need to know about me is that I am building a resume. I have had many respectable jobs, and I am going to college. Not sure what a resume will get me, but it is one of my life goals to have a full one. I also want a family and to be as good to someone else as my sisters have been to me.

Contents

Chapter 1 — August 25, 1954

Marie
Crash!

AS MY MOMMA WOULD SAY, "It is hot as hell out here." And she would be right. I can't remember a summer like this. The weather guys said we had more days over 100 degrees this summer than any other year on record. I believe it. I looked at the thermometer hanging under the crabapple tree—96 degrees. I looked at my watch to make sure it really was morning. Yep, 96 at eleven o'clock. And that's in the shade. I am standing under the canopy of the tree, fanning my face with my hand, rocking from side to side trying to create some breeze up my dress. Jimmy, my two-year-old, is pulling at my skirt. My fourth child is in my belly, and it's a heavy one.

I know we had a record-breaking hot summer two years ago, but I was not pregnant at that time. Although I seem to always be pregnant here in my adult life. I had Jimmy in June '52 before the sweltering heat settled over Raleigh. At this time two years ago, I was twenty pounds lighter than I am now. For sure this is the hottest I've ever been.

My husband, Al, likes the fact that he has a large family. But he doesn't have to carry the babies inside till he is about to explode. And he doesn't have to endure the most excruciating pain ever—giving birth. We both wanted children, but that was before I understood how much work they were. My friend Barbara and Aunt Annie make it look easy. They talk about all the fun they have with their children. Barbara says being a mother is a gift from God. Well, after this one, because it is coming whether I like it or not, I have plenty of God's gifts. He can stop with that bequest.

I'll call Momma later, as I do once a week. Maybe she can give me some new ideas about enduring this heat. I have tried all of her earlier ideas—put a cold, wet cloth around my neck and drape it down my chest, stick my head in the freezer while fanning with the church fan, drink plenty of cold water, sit down in a chair and stick my feet in the freezer, and never leave the shade during the day.

On our last call she said, "Heavens, Marie, you learned how to make ice cream at the knees of North Carolina's best ice cream maker. Keep doing it and eat it all the time. It doesn't matter how fat you get right now, you got three kids and one more coming any day. Nobody's looking at your figure."

Oh, gee thanks, Momma.

From the yard, I could hear the radio inside switching from news to songs. "We're Gonna Rock Around the Clock Tonight!" was playing. It's depressing. I will never be able to rock around the clock again, unless I am up nursing a baby. I don't remember the last time I slept all night. Another song comes into my head. One that is more what I want. Doris Day's song, "I'll See You in My Dreams." Yeah, that's what I wish for.

I was shaken from my dreams by a thunderous noise. The ground actually shook. It sounded like a tree falling or cars crashing. Or a tree coming down on a car. I grabbed Jimmy's hand and ran around the house to the front yard. Sure enough, there was a car turned on its side in the deep ditch in front of our house. There was smoke billowing from its hood.

My feet stopped like I had reached the edge of a ravine and if I took one more step we'd fall into a bottomless pit. I jerked Jimmy's arm swinging him off his feet, propelling him behind my back. Jimmy shrieked, "Momma, no!"

I hoisted Jimmy on my hip and carried him to the front door of the house. Shouting at my children inside, I yelled, "Al! Mary! Come get your brother!"

I could hear the children running toward the front of the house. I opened the door and practically tossed Jimmy inside. "Stay in there, children. You hear?"

Slamming the door behind me, I ran toward the car. The neighbors must have heard the crash or Jimmy's shout. At least a half dozen people were sprinting into our yard—mostly women. The men were at work.

Even though I didn't want to, I ran toward the car. I stopped short. I recognized the car. "Oh my God, no!" I screamed.

I could not make my feet move. The red Buick convertible had its top down. The man in the driver's seat was slouched forward. His head was on the huge steering wheel. Blood was everywhere—on the dashboard, windshield, and gushing from wounds on his head. I didn't know for sure who it was because his face was turned away from me. He was not moving. I could not see a rise and fall of his chest. He did not seem to be breathing. I wanted to vomit.

Finally, I began to run toward the car, forgetting the fear of what might be true. "Frank! Oh dear God, Frank!" I shouted so loud I hoped to literally wake the dead.

The car was so long I didn't run around to the driver side. I climbed over the passenger side where the window was down and reached toward the man. I wanted to pull his head up so I could see his face.

My next-door neighbor Barbara yelled to me. At first I didn't hear everything she said, but then I heard her say, "Marie, get back! The car might blow!"

She ran to me and grabbed my waist trying to pull me away from the car. But I was too heavy for her. I had already lifted my girth over the car door and grabbed the man's shoulders and turned his head toward me. It felt like I was struck by lightning. My heart and head were going to explode.

"FRANK! FRANK! NO!"

Then I shrieked so loud I could be heard over others who were shouting orders to the growing crowd. "Call the police! He needs an ambulance right now!"

Barbara began taking charge. "Sally, go back in the house and call the police! We can manage this out here.

"Everyone, get water! Plenty of it! We need to put out the fire.

"Alice, Jackie, help us pull this guy out and away from the car."

Running to the driver's side, Barbara commanded, "Marie, get down from there! We'll get him from this side."

I managed to pull myself off the door and then collapsed on the ground. My body was too heavy to move. The noises around me were losing their volume. I heard nothing except my own desperate howling. "Frank! No, Frank! NO! Please hang on! Frank, you must not leave me! You can't leave my family! You can't leave Momma!"

I stirred when I heard the sirens. My children were lying around me on the grass weeping and moaning.

Al Jr held his head gently against mine, whispering in my ear. "Mommy, are you all right? Are you hurt? You're scaring Jimmy. Please stop crying."

My responsibilities motivated me to come back into the world. I could not get up or even open my eyes. I felt heavier than I really was.

My middle child, Mary, the compassionate one, said, "I need a hug, Mommy."

I heard Barbara's voice. "Marie, lay still. Children, come over here with me. I have plenty of hugs to give."

I could tell someone was touching me and asking me questions. As I sank into a dark tunnel, I heard Grandma Flo speaking, "Hang on, sweet girl. Hang on."

CHAPTER 2 — AUGUST 25, 1954

Barbara Liberman
Women to the Rescue

A BOOM AND A COLOSSAL crack of a tree happened very close to my house. I hesitated to get up and go to the window. I was sitting in the only place in my house where it was cool. I had rigged the standing electric fan in front of the open refrigerator door and had just gotten my body temperature lowered to a point where I would not pass out. The children were napping. This was Me Time. Cool Me Time. Someone else will take care of what just happened out there.

Then I heard my neighbor Marie, yelling, "FRANK! FRANK! NO!"

It was a desperate yell, one that comes from the gut. I jerked the fan's cord from the wall socket, yanked the fan away from the refrigerator, and slammed its door.

I tiptoed to my children's bedroom door and opened it for a peek inside. The boys were fast asleep. I watched long enough to see their chests rise and fall.

"Kids are lucky. They can sleep through anything," I mumbled. The overhead fan was blowing on them. That rhythmic spin of the fan blades and the bounce of the chain hanging down lulled them into a deep sleep.

I went back to the kitchen and squirmed my bare feet into my sandals. Then I rushed toward the front door. I was careful opening and closing the screen door, so I would not wake the children. I hadn't yet let myself look at what might be outside.

I squinted against the blistering sun to verify what I thought I had heard. Marie, who is eight or nine months pregnant, had hoisted herself over the passenger side of a wrecked car, trying to reach the person in the driver's seat. She was crying and moaning words I could not make out. I ran to her, trying to pull her backside from the car. I yelled, "Marie, get down from there!"

She seemed to be stuck on the edge of the open window. I yelled again. "Marie, get down from there! You are going to hurt yourself and the baby! The car is smoking! It might blow!"

Marie let go of the seat of the car and collapsed to the ground like Jell-O falling from a dish. I put my hand in front of her nose and felt her breathing. Then I grabbed one of the buckets of water that the women were bringing and rushed over to douse the front of the car.

"Well, that was stupid," I said to no one really.

Then more loudly, I reminded us all, "We have to throw the water under the hood. We are not washing the dang car! We need to get the water on the engine! Give me another bucket!"

Just like I was watering one of my fine lilies, I carefully poured the water where the hood was bent open. The sizzling sound told me I had found the right spot. Two other neighbors poured their buckets of water the same way.

I put my hands on my hips and stared at the tree. It was a strong one, but it had splintered. The broken part of the tree was leaning toward the car. The weight of the splinted tree top was going to make it topple before long—right on the car.

I thought I heard sirens in the distance. I looked in the direction of the sound, but I could see nothing. I was hoping the ambulance was not going somewhere else.

Remembering that Marie was still on the ground, I circled the car to get back to her. All of a sudden, the door to her house slapped open, and her children were running toward her quiet body. The children were shrieking like wild animals. They ran and fell all around her, begging her to get up. She began moving her head slowly like she was trying to wake up from a long nap. Since she was responding to the children's cries, I stepped back.

Then I heard different siren noises and realized that the children's cries were the first set of sirens. I looked up and down the street. Police cars were coming from two directions. An ambulance was close behind. Men were jumping out from all vehicles and running toward the car. By this time the driver had been pulled out of the car and lay on the street several feet from danger.

A medic saw Marie on the grass and came running to her. He placed two fingers on her neck and the stethoscope on her protruding belly. He asked me, "Was she in the car at the time of the crash?"

I shook my head, but realized that I really didn't know. He shouted to the other medic, "We need another ambulance. This woman needs to go to the hospital."

The children's crying got louder and more frantic.

I dropped to the ground next to Marie and her children. While the medic was checking Marie, Mary asked her mother for a hug. Mary and I both were hoping Marie would respond. She did not, so I pleaded to the children, "Come here to me. I have plenty of hugs to give."

Mary came first and put her sweet arms around my neck. Then Jimmy crawled over and lay his head on my lap. Al hesitated looking from me to his momma, then asked the medic, "Can you help her? She has our baby inside her. Daddy needs Momma and all his children."

I was flabbergasted that this seven-year-old understood the danger. He was just a child himself but thinking like an adult.

The medic must have thought the same thing. "Son, we are going to make sure your next baby brother or sister and your momma are okay. What's your name?"

"Al Jr. I'm named after my daddy."

"Well, Al Jr, my name is William. I need your help now so we can care for your mother. Can you take your sister and brother with your neighbor here and wait until your daddy comes home?"

Al Jr looked at me as if to get permission for the plan.

I nodded my head. "Of course, Mr. William. We'll all go inside and have some lemonade. Come, children, let's get out of this heat."

The medic mouthed to me without making a sound, "Please call their father."

I nodded again and silently responded that I would.

He spoke to the children, "We're going to Mary Elizabeth Hospital where the doctors and nurses will give the best care to your mother and your baby."

Mary wanted more assurance. Looking up from our hug, she asked, "Mrs. Liberman, will Momma be all right?"

I was hoping to be able to give Mary, Al, Jimmy, and me that reassurance. "You heard the good man. She will have the best care. In the meantime, we will take care of each other. I'll bet your daddy will get over to the hospital quickly, and he can help her get well too."

The children and I got up. We were all a little shaky. I reached an arm over all three sets of shoulders, trying to keep them moving forward. Tears were flowing down my face. Al Jr grabbed Jimmy's hand and then Mary's. We walked slowly. Nobody wanted to look back at the very still body of their mother.

I brought the children to my front stoop and kneeled to be within inches of their sweet faces. "Daniel and Stephen are sleeping. So, let's take a moment and pray for your mother and the man in the car. God may be busy. Let's call him up to make sure the doctors and nurses have the power to do their job."

All three children went down to their knees and put their hands together in prayer.

I don't know enough prayers for the Christian God. But mine is nearly the same. I prayed as I would to every God.

"Dear God, I ask that you wrap your arms around Marie and the man. They are hurt and need the power of your love on them and those who treat them. Lord, these are good people. Heal them! Amen."

Al Jr spoke up. "And angels watch them through the night and wake up with the morning light."

Mary looked at her brothers and said, "Amen."

My heart was full. These children are blessed with a good mother.

I didn't want to startle my two sleeping boys, so I quietly opened the screen door and then the inside door.

Looking at the children, I put my finger to my lips. They rose silently and entered my house. I turned to see two medics loading Marie onto a gurney. She was still and her eyes were closed.

Marie's fine children plopped on the couch all bunched together. There was not a sound in the room except my sandals swishing on the wood floor. I walked to my sons' bedroom, gently turned the knob, and pushed the door open enough to see them. They were lying on the bed, with no sheet covering them, staring at the ceiling fan.

Daniel, the oldest, said, "What happened out there, Mother? Did anyone die?"

I sat on the side of the bed and leaned over to

cover both boys in my hug. "No. No one died. There was a car crash, and Mrs. Roberts tried to help the man in the car. You know she is carrying a baby. She just did too much. The ambulance took Mrs. Roberts and the man in the car to the hospital. The Roberts children are in the living room. They will be staying with us for a while.

"I want you to go make the Roberts children feel welcome. I'm going to get some lemonade for all of you and then make some telephone calls. Come on now."

Ethel
Life Interrupted

I AM SICK AND TIRED of packing boxes. It's nuts how much stuff we have. I stink to high heaven because it is hot as hades and I've been sorting and packing all day! I never thought I could sweat this much.

All of a sudden, the smell made me flash back to being a child. Daddy would come in the house hot and sweaty after working in the field or in the barn. Momma would say to him, "James, you are sweatin' like a pig, and you smelled like one too." He always replied by giving Momma a big sweaty hug. She would squeal like a kid.

I chuckled to myself. Daddy's been gone over thirty-seven years. Even today I still use *sweatin' like a pig*. That younger sister of mine, Annie, likes to put me in my place about it. Every chance she gets, she speaks up, "Ethel, really! Pigs don't sweat. In fact, they don't have sweat glands. You know that!"

She knows how to spoil a good saying.

Larry and I are taking a gigantic risk. We've decided to move to the coast of North Carolina and open another business. We've been running The Kooler Ice Cream Shop and Washerette in Burlington since before my sister Dianne died. Her daughter, Suzy, became our daughter after Dianne's death. Suzy is really good at managing the business. She has been learning at my shoulders for years. She's a big help because I've been traveling a lot to Washington, DC, to visit Annie, the middle Nash sister. Now that Marie and Al are settled in Raleigh, I can take longer trips and check in on her and my baby sister, Caroline, the other Raleighite. Two stopovers in one trip. In my absence, Suzy has shown she has a head for business.

When Larry and Suzy were running The Kooler and Washerette while I was working through challenges with Caroline and Annie, they paid off more of the bills than I'd done. Suzy is smart and likes figuring out the next service we can give those that bring us their dirty laundry.

At least once a month Larry and me have Suzy and Marie over for a Sunday family dinner. If Al is not around to watch my grandbabies, Marie brings them too. At the last dinner we had together the beginning of August, Al took the children to his mother's house. Even when we don't have a lot in the cupboard, I cook whatever. Last time we were together it had to be chicken backs and rice. Since we had a bumper crop of green beans and tomatoes this year, I added those to the meal. Not fancy food but it turned out okay.

On that night, as I was getting up to get coffee, Suzy asked me to sit a while longer.

"Momma. Larry. I have a new business idea. You know my friend Francie. She can sew and does amazing alterations on all kinds of clothes. I've seen her remake a plain dress into something spectacular! Since people are getting richer and lazier, we can wash, dry, iron, and alter their fancy garments. I asked some customers if they would use that service. All of them said yes. Most women don't even want to use their sewing machine anymore."

Marie was first to announce her delight. "That's a terrific idea, Suzy!"

She grunted as she stood from the table and twirled. "I am getting bigger and bigger with baby number four. The clothes I wore for babies one and two and three are too small. I'm patching them with panels of fabric to get them around this ever-widening-big-as-a-whale body. And when I get skinny again after this baby, I will need to alter my clothes down. I don't have the money that Auntie Annie has to get her clothes fixed to fit her tiny body, but maybe I can get a sister discount at The Kooler Ice Cream Shop and Washerette."

Suzy, Larry, and I laughed loudly at Marie's description of her body and her ulterior motive for adding this new service.

The giggling quieted. I chimed in. "Well, I'll be, Suzy! That is a really good plan. My generation was trained to sew. We had to. There was no other way. But not all people are good at it. In fact, you can look at people anywhere and see who shouldn't be sewing their own clothes. If your lady is as good as you say she is, we could bring her the business and charge the customer fifty percent more. This lady would never have to go after customers again."

Larry put his thumb and first finger on his chin and cocked his head. He was looking at the ceiling as if there was another idea up there. "Ethel, this proves it! Suzy is just as good or maybe even better at running this business in Burlington than we are! Now we can do what we've always wanted. Let's turn the shop over to Suzy and move to the beach!"

He gently slapped me on the backside and yelled just like a cowboy might when he wants his horse to get the heck outta here. "Let's giddy-up, Ethel!"

When Larry first talked about this last summer, it was just a foolish notion to me. But Larry was not backing down on his idea. Any chance he got he would tell me more about Topsail Island, NC, and why it was a good idea to close the business and move there. It wasn't until he proposed that we open a second branch of The Kooler and Washerette down there that I began to listen. Larry kept flattering me by reminding me how much I liked being a business woman and how good I was at it.

A year after the idea was brought up, he was able to open a crack in my closed mind. I remember the words of his persuasive argument. He said, "Ethel, hear me out. The army owned Topsail Island, and now they have left. There are civilians around there getting property for little money. The town of Surf City was started in '49 and as each year goes by, more and more people want to buy property for second homes at a ree-sort."

After the slap on my backside and his giddy-up, that ree-sort comment came back to mind. I looked at him like I looked at Al Jr when he brought his grandma some flowers he picked from the yard. Larry had softened me. Again, I see how smart he really is. He's a good man. I know that even when he makes me do things I would rather not. So, here I am at nearly midnight packing boxes in Burlington to move to Surf City.

The telephone rang—just once. My body jerked at the noise, and I yelled "HEL-LO!" into the thin air.

Usually, I throw out a cuss word or something when the telephone interrupts my work, my thinking, or when I'm in the can. But this time I was just startled. Who would be calling at almost midnight?

I rushed to the kitchen to pick up the telephone receiver. I positioned myself right in front of the electric fan, figuring I might need it.

"This is Ethel. What's happening?"

"Mrs. Ethel Martin?" The man at the end of the line sounded very serious.

"Yeah, who wants to know?"

"This is Doctor Harold Ellis at Mary Elizabeth Hospital in Raleigh. Do you have a few minutes to talk?"

My throat dried up and swelled like there was a sock in it. I started trying to clear it like a cat with a hairball.

The voice tried again. "Ma'am, are you all right? Can you hear me?"

I said, "Just wait just a dang minute." I let the phone cord and the receiver drape to the floor and stepped to the kitchen sink. I grabbed the first glass I could reach. It wasn't clean, but that didn't matter. I filled it with water and gulped it down. I grabbed the telephone receiver.

"I'm okay. I just don't like conversations that start with "this is doctor so-and-so." Who are you calling about? Caroline? Marie? Or my grandchildren? I know you ain't calling about Larry. He's right here."

Larry walked into the room. There are many times that phone rings with bad news, and Larry has to help me make out what the person is trying to say. A call this late would get his attention. He stared right at me and raised his eyebrow in that what-the-hell-is-happening-now way he does.

The doctor started again. "I'm sorry to disturb you this late. I'm a doctor at Mary Elizabeth Hospital in Raleigh, and I'm calling about Marie Nash Roberts. She was admitted . . ."

Now I interrupted him, "Lawd! Did Marie have that baby already? It's way too soon! Is she okay? I don't know why she didn't call me."

Larry leaned toward me and the telephone and said, "Geez, Ethel, let the man talk!" He put his hand over mine on the receiver to tilt it so we both could hear.

"Mrs. Roberts is in our hospital in intensive care. So far, the baby is okay. There was a car crash. The police are not sure if she was in the car, but that does not matter. We are also treating a Mr. Frank Pollard in another wing of the hospital. We just wanted to know if you are next of kin for both Mr. Pollard and Mrs. Roberts."

I yelled, "WHAAAT? What are you saying? My dear babies! Where are the rest of my babies? Oh Lord, help us all!"

My legs could not hold me. My lungs filled with air, but wouldn't let me exhale. I dropped to the kitchen floor. I could hear nothing else except the horrible moan that was coming from me. The room began to spin. Then all went dark and quiet.

Chapter 4 — August 26, 1954

Caroline
Being the Helpful One

BARBARA LIBERMAN CALLED LATE LAST night and told me about Marie and Frank. She lives next door to Marie. I've never met her, but I know a lot about her. When Marie comes to see me at Dix Hill, Barbara keeps the kids. I don't know how much she knows about me, but for some reason she thought I could help. Maybe because I live in Raleigh she thought I could be the quickest one to get to Marie. Barbara couldn't go because she had Marie's three children and her own two boys.

Right now I am sitting outside Dr. Tom Redmond's office to talk about me being able to leave campus. It's early, but he has always said, "Visit whenever you need to, Caroline."

Mrs. Teresa Mills, his secretary, called him, but he was not at the phone number she used. "Caroline, are you feeling anxious or afraid? If I cannot reach Dr. Redmond, I can call another doctor or nurse. You are welcome to wait here where it is safe. Can I get you some water? A cup of tea?"

I thought, what a stupid question, but I said, "Yes, I am anxious. Something has happened to my niece and my family lives out of town. I need to go to Mary Elizabeth Hospital because no one else can! I tried to go last night, but the house mother said I don't have permission to leave. She said I need to be escorted. Well, there is no escort! I have a car. With directions, I can get there."

I could tell my voice was getting *hostile*. The therapists here have used that word for decades, saying "Don't let your voice get hostile; it raises your blood pressure."

When I would raise my voice, Ethel would add to that reminder, "And coming from you, Caroline, it scares people!" That's the point we usually laugh.

Thinking of Ethel, I smiled to myself. I calmed my voice. "Do you know who qualifies as an escort? That's all I really want to know. I don't need Dr. Redmond if you can help me get to my niece."

The outer door of the office opened, and Dr. Redmond greeted Mrs. Mills. "It is going to be a good morning, Teresa! The sunrise is the color of orange marmalade. And the temperature feels a little cooler."

I had never heard Dr. Redmond talk about things like that. He is always so . . . clinical. Weird. I stood to make sure he knew I was there, and he wouldn't get any weirder.

Mrs. Mills beat me to it. "Dr. Redmond, Caroline Nash needs to speak with you. She is waiting there."

She pointed at me standing in front of his inner office door.

When he saw me, his body straightened a little. His voice went back to *Doctor* Redmond. "Caroline, it's good to see you. Are you feeling okay? What can I help you with?"

I ran my hands through my hair to make sure it was not crazy looking. Then used my hands mostly to press down my skirt but also to make sure nobody could see them trembling.

Dr. Redmond said, "Give me a couple of minutes to get settled. Then come into my office so you can tell me what's worrying you."

Mrs. Mills stood and gestured for me to sit down. She picked up her pad of paper and pen then followed him into his office, closing the door behind her. I guess she was telling him about the hostile voice I was using.

It took more than a few minutes for Dr. Redmond to settle. I could hear their voices but not what they were saying. I began thumping my heel on the floor, a nervous move that worried people when they saw me do it. The door opened, and my heel froze to the floor.

"Caroline, Dr. Redmond can see you now. May I bring you something to drink? I am getting coffee for the doctor."

I stood and summoned my adult-not-crazy voice. "Yes, please. Coffee with sugar and milk. Thank you."

"Come in, Caroline." Dr. Redmond said.

I sat in a big, brown leather chair in front of his desk. I never felt anything but small in that chair. Today was even worse. I squirmed to get my bottom to fit in the back of the chair, but my feet stuck straight out because the bend of my knees was on the flat cushion. I scooted forward so my legs could bend. Sitting straight up was required, so that didn't work either. I had to ask him permission to leave the campus, but looking like a 10-year-old was not going to convince him I was grown-up enough.

Dr. Redmond was standing beside his desk. He pointed to a table and two chairs and said, "Caroline, why don't we sit over there. We might be more comfortable."

I scrambled up and went to the wooden chair. "Oh geez, yes. This is much better."

Then I started in. "You know my sister, Ethel. She lives in Burlington. And her daughter Marie lives in Raleigh. I am not sure you have ever met Marie, but she visits me all the time because she is very close by. Last spring, she brought her kids, and we all played under the big oak trees on the hill. They had such a good time running up and down the hills. Before they left, they picked two handfuls of wildflowers. One for me and one for their momma. I was so happy they got to see where I live."

Dr. Redmond was really listening, but I did not think what I was saying was important enough to use his time. "Oh well, that is not what I needed to tell you. Sorry about that." My hands were in my lap, but they were hanging on to each other tightly.

"I like hearing about your family, Caroline. They are such good people."

"Here is the bad part, Dr. Redmond. Something happened to Marie, and she is in the hospital here in Raleigh. They can't reach Ethel, but Marie's next-door neighbor called me here and told me Marie needed someone with her. Barbara, that's the neighbor, couldn't go to the hospital because she was keeping both her children and Marie's. Well, Dr. Redmond, I decided this is my turn to be the helpful one. I have decided I will go to Mary Elizabeth Hospital and be with Marie. My sisters have always been there for me, no matter what. I need to be the one this time, Dr. Redmond."

No matter how hard I tried to keep it together, my throat began to close and my eyes felt hot. I could not lose it. I had to show him I was grown-up enough to do this.

He did not act like he saw me cracking up, but I know he did. He is the best doctor of psychology around. He wouldn't miss something like that.

"Caroline, I'm sorry about Marie. What happened to her? What are they treating her for?"

"I'm not sure, but according to Barbara, she collapsed in the front yard. She is carrying baby number four, and Ethel said she is big as a cow." I saw his mouth go up on one side like he was keeping back a laugh.

"Anyway, they took her away in an ambulance. There was a car wreck in front of her house, and Barbara said she thinks the driver was Marie's first father, Frank. They had to take him away in an ambulance too. It all seems so horrible."

After a quick knock on the office door, Mrs. Mills brought in the coffee and set it on the table. Both Dr. Redmond and I kept quiet while she was in the office with us. He always does that when he's "in conference." That's what he calls it when he is talking to or about the patients here. But we all know that there is no real privacy. Every single thing about me is in my file, and I am sure Mrs. Mills has read every page.

I was afraid to pick up the coffee cup. My hands might shake and make me spill it. I decided I didn't want it right now.

When the door closed behind Mrs. Mills, Dr. Redmond sipped his coffee and said, "Caroline, I understand you need to be there. I am quite impressed with your desire to help your niece. How are you planning to get there?"

I was so relieved that he was going in the direction of yes, you can go instead of no, you cannot. "I have a car, Dr. Redmond. And I know how to drive it. I drive all over campus hauling things around for the house mothers and staff. I could drive there with good directions."

"Caroline, do you have a license to drive?"

"Uh. No. But I am a good driver."

Dr. Redmond stood and said, "Give me a few minutes and let me work something out. First, I will call the hospital and see if Marie and Frank can have visitors. Please wait right here."

He left the office and closed the door behind him. I was stunned. Now that I might be able to do this, I felt nervous. Not having a nervous breakdown nervous. Just a bit scared. I rubbed my sweaty hands on my skirt and grabbed the cup of coffee. It wasn't very hot anymore, so I gulped it down all at once.

I had some quiet time to think things through. Usually, Ethel or Annie was the thinker and planner. Now it was on me. With that thought, I began to smile. It is on me. I grabbed the paper and pencil that were on the table and began writing a To Do list. That is what they would have done.

How to help my sister:
1. Get permission from Dr. Redmond.

(I put a big check mark by that one.)

2. Pack an overnight bag. (Momma told us to always take plenty of clean underwear and toiletries when visiting someone overnight.)
3. Call Ethel and tell her I am going to help Marie. Tell her to call Annie and explain that everything is under control.
4. Drive to the hospital with someone who has a license or take a taxi.
5. See if Marie and I can call Barbara and talk to the children so they know she is fine.
6. Stay as long as she needs me.

As I wrote number three, my throat closed up. When I wrote number six, the tears began to flow. I am going to be the one that can help. FINALLY.

Someone knocked softly on the door. I quickly

grabbed my handkerchief from my skirt pocket and wiped my face. Now I know why Momma insisted we always carry a handkerchief and never have clothes without a pocket.

When I felt I was presentable, I stood and said, "Come in."

Dr. Redmond came in with a note pad and sat at the table. I seated myself again, feeling very grown-up.

"Caroline, I was able to speak to a doctor at the hospital about Marie and Frank. Marie's baby is okay, but they are keeping Marie hydrated and quiet so that she will not deliver the baby right away. Marie is sleeping well but can receive visitors, especially family. She wakes every hour or so. The doctor, Dr. Harold Ellis, says it will do her good to have a short visit from a family member."

I began to feel relaxed and in control. "Dr. Redmond, is the baby going to be all right? Marie, too?"

"Yes, Caroline. The prognosis for them is good."

He paused a moment and gave me a thoughtful look. "But the news is not as positive for Frank. Dr. Ellis is not treating him. Another doctor is assigned to him. But Dr. Ellis has checked on Frank from time to time because Marie keeps asking for him. Frank sustained multiple injuries from the car crash. He is not conscious. He had surgery on broken bones. A surgeon is coming today to open his chest and examine his heart and lungs."

I listened to Dr. Redmond carefully. I can make my lungs rise and fall in good cleansing breaths whenever I get anxious. Momma and Ethel taught me that from the time I was very young. Momma would say, "Breathe deep, dear girl. Get the bad air out and bring in the good air." Ethel would just keep it simple, "Caroline, breath deep like it is your last breath." This time my body was doing it without my mind commanding it.

I turned over the piece of paper so Dr. Redmond could see my list. "I can do this, Dr. Redmond. I have started my list."

As he read it, a big smile came across his face. "Well, Caroline, it looks like you are on the right track. Go pack your bag and call your sister. That takes care of number two and three on your list, and then come back here. I think we can settle number four together and find a way for you to get to the hospital. I'm not sure if you and Marie will be able to do number five, call to speak with the children, but you can visit Marie and get enough information to call the neighbor yourself and talk to children. Just be as positive as you can be. Children need hope to lessen their worry."

I did something I had never done before. In fact, it was probably not allowed. I quickly stood from the chair, circled the table and gave Dr. Redmond a big Nash family hug. It was a good squeeze. He stood with his arms straight by his side and quietly said, "Caroline, I am very proud of you. You always have been a person your sisters could rely on. You just haven't yet had the opportunity to show them." He then raised his arms and patted me on the back. Even though it was not a full hug, it was just the one I needed.

Rushing to my house, I packed a bag and all my essentials for staying at Mary Elizabeth Hospital. I needed my medicine, a book to read, and an extra set of clothes. Dr. Redmond gave me a permission note to show the house mother so I could leave and most likely not be back tonight. After I felt organized, I called Ethel.

The telephone rang and rang. Hmm, I thought to myself. That's not like Ethel. She always picks up, even when she's mad that she has been disturbed. I hung up and tried the number again. I may have just misdialed. This time the telephone rang five times. Okay, they must be out somewhere. I decided I would try again later. My chauffer would be here in a few minutes and I needed to get to Marie.

Chapter 5 — August 27, 1954

Annie
A Change in Role

THE CHILDREN AND I WERE all doing what we loved—being in the same space doing our favorite things. Lisa was curled up in Ethel's watermelon-colored upholstered chair. I had it built to replicate a chair Ethel got from Momma when she was fifteen years old. Ethel stayed with me weeks and months at a time during my second pregnancy and after the twins were born. She spent hours of time comforting and crying with me. We talked of the unfairness of life, religion, love, and mourned the death of my baby, Thomas.

I was leafing through a *Time* magazine, trying to catch up on the world news. I was distracted by Lisa turning the pages of E.B. White's *Stuart Little*. It was one of her favorite books. I started reading it to her five years ago when she first showed great interest in chapter books. I asked her what Stuart was up to today.

She hesitated, pulling the book to her chest, and asked me if it was silly for her to be reading this at fourteen years old. At that moment I was reminded how much I and my younger sister, Caroline, like to read. I answered, "Of course not, little lady! It doesn't matter what you are reading, just never stop reading." That started a great conversation.

"I'm to the part where Stuart meets Harriet, and she is little like him. Although she looks more human than he does. Remember that part, Momma?"

"Yes, I do, Lisa. And seeing you in Aunt Ethel's chair reminds me it might be time for you to have your own thinking chair made. My momma said all women who are coming of age need a comfortable thinking and planning chair. You should look through the magazines to find a chair you might like for your thinking chair."

"That would be sooo cool, Momma!"

Jon Jr was at the desk across the room painting a model airplane. His ability to concentrate on something for so long, even though he's not yet 10 years old, was amazing. It was Jon's idea to have a carpenter build a bookshelf in Jon Jr's bedroom to display all the models he had put together. There were so many because that's all he asks for at birthdays and Christmas.

Jon Jr looks like his dad with his dark brown hair and brown eyes. And he's a lot like his daddy in other ways too. Serious, quiet, and rarely rambunctious. I appreciate that, because the youngest Walsh is never quiet. She has to be the center of attention.

I glanced at Dianne dancing to no music I could hear. She held an invisible telephone receiver to her ear and was talking with no noise. When she caught my eye she said, "Momma, haven't we had enough quiet time? Can I turn on the radio now? We need to do some Shake, Rattle, and Roll! Lisa, come on! I know you like to dance! Maybe that dreamy Eddie Fisher will sing. PLEASE, Momma!"

Trying not to giggle at Dianne. I stood up and grabbed her hand. "Okay, little girl. Let's add some fun."

I tapped Jon Jr on the head. He rolled his eyes and reluctantly allowed me to pull him out of the chair. "Let's do it, my little man. I heard about a new dance. It is called the Cha Cha Cha."

I pulled them to the middle of the floor and showed them what little I knew of the dance steps without any music playing.

"Okay, let's try. Start feet together. Move right foot forward a little step. Then left foot to meet the right. Right foot back. The left joins the right. Then three little steps in the same place. That is the Cha Cha Cha part."

As I began to hum the beat, they joined me side by side. We really didn't know what we were doing, but we were having fun. Dianne could not stop giggling. And Jon was so focused on his feet, he almost tripped over himself. Laughter filled the room. Lisa put down her book and joined us. For the next few minutes, our Cha Cha Cha turned into any way we wanted to move. I collapsed in a chair. Lisa joined me, then Dianne. To my surprise, Jon Jr was still working on his dance moves.

Trying to be encouraging without letting a giggle erupt, I said, "Jon baby, you are going to be the best dancer in the family. You work so hard on it!"

Dianne demanded, "Momma, we must have a record player! We must dance every day! Jonny needs to practice!"

Lelia, our dear nanny for more than ten years, was standing in the doorway. Her hand covered her mouth as if she was trying not to laugh. I rose from the chair, and the girls plopped to the floor. "Hello, Lelia! Come along and dance with us. Do you like to dance?"

"I do like to dance, but I never danced like that."

Jon Jr responded rather proudly, "It's called the Cha Cha Cha. It's easy. Even I can do it." Then he demonstrated a few times for her, staring down at his feet the whole time.

Lelia clapped for him. Then walking over to me, she whispered into my ear. "Mrs. Walsh, you had a phone call from a woman named Miss Liberman. Barbara Liberman. She said she lives next door to Mrs. Marie and needs to talk to you. She gave me her telephone number."

I took the small paper with Lelia's printing on it. "Did she say what this was about? Why didn't Marie call?"

"Ma'am, she didn't say. But she sounded worried."

I rushed down the hall to the telephone in my bedroom. Lelia followed me. She was evidently more worried about the call than I understood.

I dialed the number and introduced myself.

"Hello Mrs. Liberman. This is Annie Nash Walsh, Marie's aunt, calling you back. How can I help you?"

"Mrs. Walsh, I am glad I was able to reach you. I have been trying to get in touch with Marie's mother and can't seem to reach her. I have talked to Caroline Nash and she hasn't been able to reach her either. I was wondering if you might know if they have gone out of town or how I might reach her."

"Oh my, Barbara. Is it okay if I call you Barbara?"

"Certainly, I prefer it. Usually when someone calls me Mrs. Liberman I look around for my mother-in-law."

I giggled a bit, then said. "Me too. I am not old enough yet to be called Mrs. Walsh by people older than my children. I don't know where Ethel is. I spoke with her last week, but she didn't mention going out of town."

"Well, Annie, I have distressing news. Marie has been admitted to a hospital in Raleigh. There was a car accident in her front yard the day before yesterday. She was not hit by the car, as far as I know, but she experienced some distress and passed out. The man in the car that hit a big tree was badly hurt. That man was Frank, who I believe is Marie's father. An ambulance came for both of them. Caroline gave me Ethel's telephone number and asked me to continue calling her and tell her what happened. She also asked me to tell Ethel to call you. Since I have not been able to reach your sister, I went back to Marie's house and found your number."

I was stunned. I couldn't process what I was hearing. Lelia put her hand on my shoulder. It was like a guide pushing me toward my next step.

After a few deep breaths I could focus. "Barbara, is Marie all right? How about the baby she's carrying? Do you know anything about Frank? This is all too horrible."

Barbara provided some good news. "I hear that Marie and the baby are okay. The doctors have Marie resting. I don't know the details, but Al gives me reports. He drops the children with me when he goes to the hospital. He says the doctors and nurses are doing a good job with her and the baby. Today he said he was going back to work since Marie's aunts will be coming. The news is not so good for Frank. Apparently, he has had surgery and may still be unconscious."

"Well then, Barbara, Marie's aunts will indeed be heading to Raleigh. I will continue calling Ethel. I'm sure I'll be able to at least get Larry to pick up the telephone, or I will send a telegram like in the old days. Thank you so much for being there for the children. We owe you big time!"

Barbara was as comforting as Marie had described her to be. "Annie, from what I know, Mary Elizabeth Hospital is one of the best in the area. They will take good care of your niece and Frank too. Take your time. Marie needs you, but not at the risk of driving too fast."

A good reminder.

CHAPTER 6 — AUGUST 26 AND 27, 1954

Ethel
Who Cares for Whom?

I WOKE WITH THE SUN streaming through the window. I don't remember how I got into my bed. I don't really remember much from last night except getting a telephone call from a doctor in Raleigh.

I called out, "Larry, where are you? Come in here and tell me what has happened!"

I heard his feet shuffle across the wooden floors. When he entered the bedroom he responded, "Well, there she is. How do you feel? We had quite the scare last night."

"I know it was a scary call, but I don't remember much. What was it about?"

Larry sat on the side of the bed and leaned in to kiss my cheek. Uh oh, I thought. Something bad has happened or he would not be bringing out that sweet Larry.

He gave the me quick summary of the call, then slowed his voice and said, "I'm also worried but not only about the call. It's more than that. It scared me seeing you drop to the floor."

Larry took hold of my arm. "Ethel, I didn't think you were dead. But looking at you like that . . . well, something came over me. I knew at that moment I could not live without you. Ever."

I told him that I had no idea why I passed out like that. I've never been a fainter. I said, "I knew a woman who fainted every time she got really sick. One time her husband had to pick her up from the toilet when she was throwing up and had the runs at the same time. Now that is a real marriage when a man will do that for his wife. I am glad you didn't have to do that. Turns out that woman faints a lot."

Larry tried to get us back to the subject. "Ethel, I need you to see a doctor. There might be something wrong in your body to make that happen."

"Oh good God, Larry. I've got more important things to do right now! You just told me about Marie, Frank, and my next grandbaby. We gotta get to Raleigh. I have to see Marie. She needs her momma!"

"Okay, shug. But here's the deal. I've called the doctor and asked him to come by and check on you. He is on his way."

In protest, I started to get out of bed. I could barely raise my head or chest from the bed. I tried again to sit up. I didn't have the muscle for it. That made me mad.

"Help me up, Larry. We are going to Raleigh. I don't need to see any damn doctor. I just need to eat something. Sit me up and get me a glass of water."

He reached an arm under my shoulders and pulled. I didn't move enough to sit up. If Larry could lift me off the floor and get me to bed last night, he should be able to sit me up.

"Come on, Larry, try harder."

He put one arm under my legs and the other under my back. He was able to turn me and raise me to sit up. The room began to spin. I gripped the sheets and sides of the bed. I held tight. I fell backward and landed sideways on the bed.

I spoke, but not in much of a voice. "Oh dang. Let me lay here a few more minutes."

Larry left the room. I could hear him rummaging in the kitchen. He came back with a tray of food and drink.

"Drink the water first. Maybe you're just dehydrated."

He held my head up and I drank it all. It tasted like sweetness.

Someone knocked and called through the screen door. "Mr. Martin, may I come in? It's Dr. Green. Walter Green."

Larry left the room. I closed my eyes a bit hoping the room would stop spinning. All went quiet again.

After what seemed like no time at all, the doctor came in the room. I knew who he was. We see him around town all the time. I raised my head a bit to look down at myself. I hoped I was covered up in my nightgown. Trying to sound as strong as I could I said, "Hey, Dr. Green. Sorry Larry bothered you, but I am fine. Just tired is all."

He replied, "No bother at all, Ethel. Larry and I have spent the last thirty minutes or so talking about your symptoms. Let me just check you over. Larry, will you sit her up please?"

Larry sat me up and put lots of pillows behind my back. Doc put the stethoscope on my chest and listened, looked in my eyes and mouth. All those things he does when I go for a check-up.

He asked a lot of questions, and I answered as many as I could. I told him I'd been packing boxes in this heat and just did too much.

"I don't remember eating. I'm just hungry and tired. Give me a pill and let me rest a bit. I need to call my sisters. Then Larry and I are going to Raleigh. I just don't have time to be sick."

In a stern voice, Dr. Green said, "Ethel, we don't get to choose when we have time to be sick. Your body tells you loud and clear what it needs. Your symptoms are not just from hunger or thirst. Fatigue is a symptom of your body needing something it is not getting. Let me check your temperature and take some blood and see what that might be telling us. Larry, will you bring her some orange juice or sweet tea? If her blood sugar is low, that might explain some things."

In the clinical doctor voice, he began to interrogate me. "Ethel, what else is going on that is different than normal."

I started to cry. That made me mad. "Doc, I got so much on me. My baby girl is in the hospital, her daddy is too. And I am hours away from her."

"Ethel, listen to your body. What else is it telling you?"

As I was crying, the ugly kind of cry, I stammered, "The damn room won't stop spinning. My head hurts like small bombs are going off in there. And I am just so tired, I can barely raise my arms."

The doc gave me a handkerchief so I could blow my nose. Then he stuck a thermometer in my mouth. I heard the phone ring, but Larry didn't pick it up. With the stick in my mouth, I couldn't fuss at him. Doc read the thermometer, shook it, then stuck a needle in my arm. If I wasn't already laying back, I would have fainted. I hate a needle.

Then there was another needle. Not one to draw blood, but to put something in me.

Next thing I knew, I woke up in a hospital. SHIT

Larry was standing by the bed holding my hand. I focused my eyes on him. He said, "Well, there you are, girl. Welcome back to the world of the livin'."

"How long have I been out?" I could hear how hoarse my voice was.

"Ethel, you've been sleeping like a new baby about eight hours. I think the medicine the doctor gave you did the trick. Let me go tell the nurse you're awake."

While I cleared my throat, I grabbed his arm. "Don't leave me. Is Marie okay?"

"I don't know, Ethel. All I have focused on is you. I am sure she is. She's in a good hospital."

Dr. Green picked this time to enter the room. "Ethel, how are you feeling?"

"Better, Doc, better. That was magic stuff you gave me. I slept so hard!"

Just to show off, I pulled myself up to sit. Larry

cheered and clapped his hands like it was a baby's first steps. Smart aleck.

The doc searched his papers. Reading about me, I guess. He said, "Ethel, you gave Larry quite a scare. The tests didn't show anything that lots of rest and healthy eating can't fix. You have to relax. Larry said you're eager to get to Raleigh. I understand that. You need to stay here tonight. The bloodwork and urinalysis results are not quite normal. I want the nurses to watch you closely a little while longer. You were dehydrated, which could cause the headache and dizziness. Your blood sugar is low. That can happen from not eating. That condition can make you weak and fatigued. There may be other things we need to consider."

I told him I couldn't stay another night. I wanted to go home. "I can sleep at home in my own bed."

What I told myself is that I would talk Larry into packing me into the back seat of the car and driving to Raleigh.

As if Larry was reading my mind he said, "Dr. Green, I know Ethel. If I take her home, she will get in that car and drive to Raleigh. I want her strong enough to take that trip."

Then he looked at me. He knew I was furious. "Ethel, right now you don't get to decide. The doctor knows best. I don't want to fight you about this, but I will if I have to. We can go tomorrow if you keep getting better."

Tears flowed. I didn't have the power to argue.

I pleaded with the doctor. "Promise I can go

tomorrow? I'll eat and drink anything you say. Give me a headache pill and shoot me in the arm with that sleeping magic. I'll wake up like superman."

Dr. Walter Green looked at Larry then me, "That's a good compromise. We'll see how you are in the morning. I'll talk to the nurse about what you need in the next hours."

Doc left the room. Larry climbed on the bed beside me. He laid down and put his arm around my waist. "Ethel, thank you for not fighting us on this. I need you to be well. You can't help with Marie if you are sick. Your grandbabies need you to be strong. Let's get you better and then you can take care of others—like you always do."

I kissed his cheek. "Thanks for loving me, Larry."

I awoke eager to see the doctor. Where was he? They brought in breakfast, and I wolfed it down. The nurse gave me a headache pill and a big glass of water. As I was drinking, I hoped Larry noticed how perky I was.

The nurse was evidently impressed. "Mrs. Martin, it looks like you had a good night. I checked on you a few times, and you were sleeping well. You are not running a temperature and your vital signs look normal.

"Yahoo! Well then, can I go home?"

"Dr. Green will have to decide. He is making his rounds. He'll be here later. Right now I want to see if you can get up and go with me to the bathroom."

Larry got out of the chair and moved to get me.

"Mr. Martin, I want to see Mrs. Martin do it without assistance. Don't worry, I'll be right here if she struggles."

I summoned my strength, pulled myself up by the handrail on the bed, and swung my legs over the side of the bed. "Ta da!" I said proudly. "I'm healed!"

After all that got done, the nurse told Larry to go get some coffee. "Mrs. Martin is going to have a bath. You can come back in thirty minutes."

I was worried about being able to get in a bathtub, but that wasn't what she was expecting. It was a simple wash with a bowl of soapy warm water and a wash cloth. I did the private areas, she washed the bigger areas. It felt good to get cleaned up. She helped me put on a house dress that Larry must have brought from home. Clean socks and shoes and I was ready to go!

When Larry came back in, I was sitting in his chair. "How do I look, big guy?"

"You look marvelous!" he said then bent over to kiss my lips. "And you smell good too!"

They brought in another tray of food. And a Pepsi. "Yipee! Pepsi! My favorite!" I hollered like a kid.

As the laughter was going on, Dr. Green came in the room. I could tell he was holding back a laugh.

"Come on, Doc, what do you think? I look great and feel great. Can I go home?

"You do look stronger. Your vitals are better. I'm going to send some medicine with you. And yes, you can go home. I want to see you again when you get back from Raleigh. Larry, will you call my office each day and let me know how she's doing?"

Larry raised his hand to his forehead and saluted the doctor. "Yes sir, I sure will."

Larry and I went arm in arm from the hospital to the car. I began making a mental list of all I needed to do. When we arrived, I went straight to the telephone to called Annie. Lelia answered and said she had gone to Raleigh. "Me too, Lelia. I am on my way there."

I moved back to high gear, but Larry beat me to it. He had our bags packed and was loading them into the boot of the car.

Suzy brought out a picnic basket full of food. "Francie and I made you sandwiches for the road. Larry dad filled it with healthy stuff from the doctor's list. He has your medicine in his pocket. I am not in favor of you taking off so soon. I should be going to help with my sister instead of you. I wish you'd stay home a few more days."

"Suzy-Q, I am better now. I'm just tired of sleeping. I have to be with your sister. I need you to keep things going around here. I'll call and give you an update."

Larry stepped in. "Ethel, the car is packed. The gas tank is full. Are you up to riding to Raleigh?"

Happily I said, "Yeah, let's go. I might need one more bathroom trip first. I promise not to faint on the toilet. I just need to get my body moving. I wish I could talk to Annie. I feel so out of touch with this situation."

After I finished in the bathroom, Suzy took my arm and walked me out to the car. When she hugged me she said, "Be well, Momma."

The hours it took to get to Raleigh went by quick. I must have dozed off. I could hear the tire noise humming on the road. Oddly, there was no radio playing. Larry usually likes to drive with the radio on. I think it keeps him alert. When the car finally stopped, I raised my head and saw a brick building. It looked more like a fancy home than a hospital. I wondered if we were even at the right place.

Larry must have spent his driving time planning what was needed. He put an arm around my shoulders. "We're here, Ethel. Are you awake enough to go in? I thought I would drop you off and check on Al and the kids. I'll see if there would be room for us at their house and find out how we can help. I know Al must be having a hard time with Marie in the hospital, and for sure the three children need her. How's that sound?"

Larry being so comforting was hard on me. I needed to be stable enough to be the one in charge. He stands strong in tough times, but he usually lets me lead. I loved him being different right now. Besides I get wore out in times of fear. I guess it was my turn to borrow some of his strength. It's true that I needed Annie, but for now I have my Larry.

I sat up, pulling myself together, and said, "Yeah, that sounds good. I'll visit with Marie as much as I can or until they kick me out. I'll call you if I need you to pick me up. I wish my sisters were with me. We always do these things better when we're together."

I kissed his cheek and pushed open the car door.

I turned back to say one more thing. "Larry,

don't tell anyone about me being sick. I'm not the priority here. I'll explain to my family after we all get through this. Nobody needs to be worrying about me."

"Except me, Ethel. I'll never stop worrying."

———

Mary Elizabeth Hospital looked different inside than I expected. It did not have the same clinic look as all of Caroline's hospitals. I wasn't sure if that gave me more confidence in Marie's care or not. Seeing a well-dressed lady sitting behind a reception-type desk reminded me of a hotel clerk rather than check-in for an infirmary.

I stood tall trying to look composed as I approached. "I am here to see Marie Roberts. A Dr. Ellis called to tell me she is here and that I should come. Where can I find her? I am Ethel Martin, her mother, by the way."

The woman looked down at a sign-in book on the table, then stood, "Oh. Actually, someone is with her now. Her aunt, I believe. There can only be one person in the room at a time."

I replied, "I know that must be my sister Annie. She was coming from Washington, DC. Oh, never mind. I get first priority. Being the momma. Can my sister and I take turns? I'll go to the room and let Annie come out."

"Yes, you can take turns. I can have someone tell her to come downstairs. Marie Nash Roberts is in room 324. Let me call the nurse assigned to her."

I walked around the entry area that actually looked like a living room in a fancy house. I could tell the building was H-shaped, but I wasn't sure which way to go. I was looking for a coffee pot brewing someplace. The reception lady must have read my mind.

"May I get you something while you wait?" she asked, sounding more like security than trying to be helpful.

I withdrew a bit. "Yes. I am looking for some coffee. Is there any around here? I have had a long drive, and I need a little pick-me-up. Is coffee allowed?"

"Certainly. When your sister comes down, I can get both of you a cup and a little something to eat. That way you can catch up. I'm sure you have a lot to talk about. You may use the office across the hall."

"I won't need time to talk. I just need a cup of joe to take up to see Marie."

I heard footsteps coming from the left hall. Hoping it was Annie, I walked toward the sound.

I froze, confused. Rather than seeing my sister with dark, curly hair, there was my sister with brown hair. "Caroline? What? What are you doing here? How did you get here?"

She ran to me and wrapped me in a strong hug. I pulled back and looked at her face, making sure this was not a crazy moment and she had broken out of Dix Hill.

"I am here to support my sisters! I am here to be with Marie. She's napping right now." She had tears in her eyes. "Ethel, I am here to be helpful instead of being the one who always needs your help."

A wave of something washed over me. I was not sure if it was fear for the Caroline I have always known. The one who can't be independent. Or if it was confusion about how this might have come about. Or deep love for her to do this, no matter how. Or was it all of that? I hugged her back and gave her a kiss on her cheek. I stepped back from Caroline and grinned. "You look good, little sister. Really good."

I looked at the reception lady and said, "We'll take that coffee in the office. You're right. We have a lot to talk about."

Caroline grabbed my hand, and like Dorothy and the Scarecrow in the *Wizard of Oz* movie, we skipped to the office. "While Marie is resting, we can talk about the details and what I have arranged."

At that point I knew what washed over me was love—Nash sister love.

Annie
Surprise!

WHEN BARBARA CALLED AND TOLD me about the accident, it scared the bajeebies out of me. The fact that Marie and Frank were in the hospital in Raleigh sent me into high gear. What's worse, nobody could find Ethel. The phone was out or something. She probably didn't know about Marie yet. I needed to get to Raleigh ASAP. We Nash sisters didn't leave each other alone in times like this.

I've never arranged a trip so quickly in my entire life. I have a new appreciation for my sister's ability to drop things and come at my beck and call. And I have done plenty of *beck and calls* (as Ethel says) in my lifetime already. I can only remember one time when she needed me. That was to help prepare our momma's funeral and handle the family estate. Even then, it still took me days to get home to help.

After I hung up from talking to Barbara, I tried Ethel again and again. Where the heck was she?

Hopefully someone reached her and she had already left for Raleigh.

The details of what happened were still swimming in my brain. It was horrific all the way around. Marie passing out, Frank being so badly hurt—possibly dead, Marie's dear sweet children having to witness their momma taken away in an ambulance, and their dad nowhere around. Thank God for good friends like Barbara. She kept Marie's children so Al was able to go directly to the hospital.

Barbara found my telephone number written on Marie's telephone pad. Of course Ethel and Suzy's number was not listed. That had also been Marie's number a good part of her life. But thank goodness she had put the number to reach Caroline on the pad, so Barbara and Caroline connected soon after the accident. My worry was that Caroline might not be able to deal with this kind of trauma.

There are good people my world. I thank God for Jon and Lelia every day. Right now, I realize I don't thank them enough. Jon got the car ready for a trip and managed to find a place for me to stay.

Lelia said, "Like in the prayers we say to God, put all the worries in my hands."

I did place my schedule, house, and children in her charge. Everything. Even when I tried to tell her what was needed, Lelia reminded me, "Mrs. Walsh, I been caring for you and this family for nearly ten years. You taught me good. We got this. Go take care of Sister."

I had trouble packing a suitcase. I had no idea how

long I would need to be there. After I stuffed the first bag, Jon walked in the room. "I have no idea what to take. I could be there a week or two weeks. I'm determined to give Ethel as much time as she would give me." Then I switched my guilt. "Jon, I haven't been away from the children like this before. Will y'all be okay without me?"

He came over and wrapped his strong arms around me. "Annie, I don't know how we will do without your love in this house, but I am sure we can manage the things we will need to do. I plan to shorten my work days while you're gone so Lelia can have a break. You're doing exactly what you should right now. The Nash sisters stick together, right?"

I stepped away from the hug and kissed his luscious lips. Geez, how did I get so lucky with this guy?

I pulled out another suitcase and started looking for more to put in it. Jon reminded me, "You know, Annie, whatever you might need, you can buy in Raleigh. I stuffed your pocketbook with lots of money. And I can send more if you need it."

The car was pulled to the front of the house, and Jon finished loading it for me. Lelia brought out a basket covered in a blue cloth. "Mrs. Walsh, here is a little something to eat along the way. And cookies for those little ones who miss their momma." My eyes began to fill with tears.

Lisa said, "Yeah, and Lelia said we will make some more cookies today for us who will miss our momma too."

Jon Jr chimed in, "And Papa is going to take us to

the hobby shop on Saturday. We can buy some things to keep us busy. Guess what I'm gonna get?"

I ruffled his hair and said, "Oh, I'm not sure. Maybe an airplane kit?"

I gave kisses to everyone, even Lelia. She is not a fan of my kisses, but she tolerates them. Once while wiping the affection from her face, she told me that kisses were for children and husbands.

After I got into the car, my tears flowed. All my DC family were waving goodbye. As I pulled away, I could hear them shouting, "See you later, alligator!"

I yelled back, "After a while, crocodile!" They were going to be fine.

I chose to drive my car to Raleigh. It made no sense to take the train. I enjoy driving because I am in control of my time. Route 1 is familiar to me. They say it can take you from New York to Florida. I would never do that by car. That is the kind of trip for the train. I am happy to use the time driving to appreciate the land around me. It reminds me of home. Cities like DC, with people hustling and bustling around, require a faster life. Driving through Virginia and into North Carolina brings the enjoyment of a slower and calmer life. Noticing the houses, stores, and people along this road makes me wonder what their stories might be. This kind of drive reminds me how much I miss home. My children would love living this kind of life. Not sure if Jon would. He likes his job and the pace of our nation's capital.

When I reached the North Carolina line, I pulled into a café for a bite to eat and to stretch my legs.

Looking at the back seat, I expected to see my children there. I got angry and shouted, "Why the hell do I live so far away from my sisters! Jon and I must move to Raleigh!"

As I opened the door of my brand new, wonderfully air-conditioned car, I realized the air outside was unbearable. It was heavy with humidity and as hot as the tropics. I would need to strip down. I climbed into the backseat of the car and closed the door. The sweater came off. I pulled off the stockings and wished I had a pair of short pants and short sleeve blouse to change into. Those were in my suitcase in the boot of the car. I'd have to manage without them. My goal now was to get through this stop quickly and let my '53 Chrysler Imperial keep me cool for the next three hours. When Jon bought the car for me, I didn't understand how essential air-conditioning would be. I was mostly impressed with the electric windows and the car's beautiful burgundy wine color. He probably fully understood.

I knew Raleigh pretty well, but I had never been to this hospital. I had the address, but no street map of the city. Once I entered the city limits, I pulled into a filling station. When the attendant came to the car, I pushed the button to roll down the window. The heat came rushing in even this late in the day.

That feature was not lost on the young man. "Shazam, ma'am! This is one nifty car! You got air conditioning in there?"

He paused to look over the outside and inside of the car, then apparently decided he better do his job.

"What can I do for you today? Fill 'er up? Oil change? I can wipe the road dust off."

When I need to, I can be a bit flirty. This was a good time to use those charms. I looked into his eyes and said, "Well, look at you, young man. You can certainly do something for me today. I have driven over five hours, and the car and I are tired. But we don't have a lot of time. So please give her as much fuel as she will take and check her out under the hood. While you do that, I'll go in and buy a soft drink for each of us."

He opened the door for me and stood back as if he were showing me into an elegant restaurant. I played into it and let my bare legs slowly reach to the ground.

He noticed. "Wowsa! You are a peach!"

I smiled at him. I was going to get the royal treatment for my looks. I went inside the station and searched for a Raleigh map, a soda, and a pack of peanuts. I like dropping peanuts into the soda bottle. It makes the drink salty and sweet. I decided to get several drinks to take to my sisters. And of course, I got an extra for the attendant.

I noticed he was wiping down the outside of my car. I've never had that done before at a filling station. They always clean the windshield, but this young man cleaned all the other windows too. What a payoff!

He walked back into the station. "She's all ready for you now. Full tank. Did you know that's a twenty-gallon tank? I've never seen one of those before. And she needed most of that. I topped off the oil and cleaned her up for you. Anything else you need?"

I handed him the soda. "Thank you for this good service. How much do I owe you?"

He rang up the bill on the cash register. "$5.00 for the fuel, twenty-five cents for the oil. So that is $5.25. The clean-up is on me. I just had a ball touching that body." He grinned a little too friendly.

I handed him a ten to cover the snacks too. His eyes grew as big as saucers. Money makes people helpful. Even more than charm. "One more thing. I need to get to Mary Elizabeth Hospital and then to a place to stay named Yellow Gables. Could you draw the directions on this map?"

"Well, ma'am, you are lucky, because both are just a few miles down this road. I'll show you on the map, but it's real easy. Just keep going south on Route 1. This road goes by both places. But look out real close. That hospital looks more like where a rich man lives than a hospital. There's a sign out there, but you might pass it. And Yellow Gables is a stone building that looks like it should be in the mountains. And there is an electric sign out front.

He drew a circle on the map for his station, then an H shaped box for the hospital, and a bed for the lodge.

I was relieved. "That is just perfect! I hope you've never had to go to the hospital yourself or to see somebody hurt. Have you ever stayed at Yellow Gables? Is it nice?"

"No, ma'am, never been to those places. But I seen 'em from the road. You have a good visit in Raleigh, and when you need fuel again, come right back here."

I thanked him and got back in the car where the air would be cool again.

It only took a few minutes to get to Mary Elizabeth Hospital. Merle, that was the name sewn on his shirt, was right. It looked like a red brick mansion. There were handcrafted wooden doors at the entryway. The evening sun was low in the sky. Long shadows were cast on the building from the trees. I could imagine young ladies in stylish dresses holding the arms of young men in black suits entering for a debutant ball. I looked at my clothing and wondered if I was going to be underdressed.

The lobby was large and very busy. It looked like a hotel lobby with comfortable chairs and small tables arranged randomly throughout the room. People were coming in, milling around, and finding places to sit. There were few people leaving. I looked around for somebody familiar. I prayed that Ethel knew what had happened and had already arrived. As I crossed the room to speak to the receptionist, I heard someone call out, "Annie! Annie Nash! Over here!"

I tried to locate the voice, but the crowd of people distracted me. It was a bit unnerving to hear someone call me Annie Nash. No one calls me that anymore. I stood still, hoping the person would call out again.

I felt a hand on my back. "Annie, it's me. Caroline." I turned and sure enough it was Caroline. I was stunned trying to understand this. I can't remember the last time I saw Caroline outside of the Dix campus.

Caroline put her hands on my shoulders and helped me get over my confusion. "Annie, it really is me. I'm helping out with Marie and Frank. Ethel is in the room with Marie. They only let one in at a time. Al is at Marie's house with the children and Larry's there too. I planned with Ethel that I would be here when you arrived. I can tell you everything. I've been here keeping watch on Marie for a while now."

I put my hands over hers. I didn't know how to process this, but just wanted to hold on to her. I was so glad to know that Ethel was here. "Oh, Caroline, that is so wonderful of you. How did you get here? Where are you staying? Do they know . . ."

"Yes, Annie, Dr. Redmond knows. He even brought me here the first day. Then he helped me arrange for a ride back and forth while I'm helping Marie. It's not that far. I told him I could drive it, but I haven't made time to get a license. Anyway, I did the right thing. I worked it all out."

She reached into the pocket of her skirt and pulled out some papers. As she was unfolding them, she said, "Ethel was as surprised as you to see me escape the looney bin. I have it all right here. I can tell you much more about this. We'll talk about Marie first. Let's find a place to sit. Then you can go up and relieve Ethel."

Caroline spotted several empty chairs on the other side of the room and pulled me toward them. "Annie, this will work. We can talk here without worrying about anyone hearing the gory details."

We talked nearly an hour. Actually, Caroline talked. I mostly listened. I learned that Marie was doing okay, but the doctors said she needed to deliver the baby. The baby was ready. They had been waiting for Marie to get a little stronger. They said she is nearly ready now. Caroline ended her report with a happy pronouncement. "So anytime now, they might operate on her and bring us a baby!"

I was paying close attention. Not only to what Caroline was saying but to how confident she sounded. Caroline's voice was steady and her words matter-of-fact. The notes on the paper seemed to be her guide.

She then told me about Frank. "On the other hand, Frank is not doing so well. He lost a lot of blood and has had several operations. He is in surgery again today with a specialist to fix any problems in his chest. I have not seen Frank, but Ethel has a few times. He has not been conscious since the accident. It is so sad, Annie. He is a good, good man."

Then I heard a crack in Caroline's voice. She looked down at her hands in her lap. Her fingers and thumbs were rubbing the pages of her notes so hard I thought she might erase the words. Her legs began twitching. I leaned over and hugged her.

Trying to soothe us both, I agreed, "Oh, Caroline, yes. Frank is a good man. He's in good hands. Let's pray hard they can help him. Where is Elizabeth and their son, Eli? How is Elizabeth taking this?"

"That is another sad part, Annie. She won't come to see Frank. According to Ethel, she's mad. Really mad. Ethel has called her to give her updates, but she just screams at Ethel. Elizabeth even said it was Frank's own fault. That he was not thinking about his "real" family. That hurt Ethel bad. But she said she did not say anything to strike back. I'm proud of her for that."

Shaking my head, I replied, "Everyone deals with

stress differently. Elizabeth probably doesn't mean it—really. Eli is about the same age as my Dianne. He needs his daddy and both of his families in his life. This reminds me how much we need to bring the whole group together often. Just like Frank has asked us to do. Let's make that pledge, Caroline."

Caroline stood, looked past me, and put her hand on her heart. I wasn't sure if she was trying to say the Pledge of Allegiance out loud or what. That is exactly what our Caroline might do.

She stepped around me and said, "Thank God." Then she shouted to the crowd of people in the lobby, "Over here, Ethel! Look, Annie's here!"

There was Ethel. She looked several years older than when I saw her last. She seemed smaller and fragile. The skin on her face was blotchy and swollen. It scared me. I almost ran across the room to her.

"Where the heck have you been, Ethel. Nobody has been able to reach you. I was worried sick!"

I engulfed her in a soft hug. I didn't want her to break. She sobbed and quietly moaned, "Oh Annie, it is a long story. But I am here now."

I heard her mumble something into my chest I could not understand except for "Thank you."

All I could say, I did. "I'm so sorry, Ethel. I know this hurts you. I'm sorry about Marie and Frank. I'm sorry I couldn't be here right away."

Caroline moved close to us, but did not join us in that moment.

Ethel lifted her head and stepped back. A smile began on her face. Speaking loud enough for both me and Caroline to hear, she said, "Annie, aren't you so proud of Caroline. She has handled so much without me. She has walked right into this terrible situation and stood strong."

She reached out and pulled Caroline into the circle of sisters. Ethel said, "Caroline has saved the day for me and everyone else. Thank God she was here. I am so thankful we are Nash sisters."

Caroline stood straight and proud. "Yeah. Finally, I am a helper and not just the sister who needs help. Thank God is right." And then laughing, she said, "It's a miracle!"

A moment of happiness poured over us.

As if to show off, Caroline started organizing us again. "Okay, sisters, let's go outside and sit on the bench under the big tree. After we talk and sit a spell, we'll each get one more visit with Marie before I go back to The Hill and you can go to your hotel room, Annie. Ethel, I know you will want to stay with Marie like I did last night. Annie and I will get back here early tomorrow morning to give you a break to get some breakfast. Is this a good plan?"

Ethel and I looked at Caroline proudly. "Sounds like a fine plan," I said.

Chapter 8 — August 27, 1954

Ethel
Sisters Together

I HEARD MY YOUNGEST SISTER shout, "Over here, Ethel! Look, Annie is here!" When I saw them, I just stared. I could have sworn I saw something unusual around them. As they came closer, I could feel the power of our family. The air smelled like roses. Yellow roses. It was as if Momma and our sister Dianne were joining us. My eardrums were pounding softly. It seemed like the sound of many hearts beating together. I collapsed into Annie's arms moaning, "Thank you, Momma and Dianne for coming. I need y'all so much."

The crowd cleared the way as we walked arm in arm toward the front door. Two people pushed open the doors for us and held them as we went through. Caroline dipped her head and looked at each of them. "Thank you, kind people."

There was a bench under a very large oak tree in the front yard. Caroline led us there. She said, "I like this tree. It reminds me of the hundreds we have on the Dix campus. I've sat here for many hours while I was waiting for y'all to arrive and Marie was sleeping. It's comforting to be here thinking and planning."

Annie agreed. "It's like the thinking chair Momma had made for us girls when we turned fifteen. She knew we needed somewhere we could make our plans and a place just to find strength. I guess she knew we would have things to worry about too. That chair is my favorite piece of furniture in our house."

Caroline added, "I have Dianne's chair, remember? I was much older than fifteen when she died. Momma was never able to get me a chair because my room at Dorothea Dix was not big enough for it. Y'all were sweet enough to make sure I got Dianne's chair when I moved into a group home on campus." Caroline paused and added, "It gets used a lot because everybody in my rooming house has a lot to worry about."

Without intending it, out came a short giggle. "Caroline, you are the funniest person I know. In the middle of crisis, you make us laugh."

Annie leaned her head on my shoulder and started to hum. We love singing, but we are not very good at it. We are better at humming. She was humming "America the Beautiful." Caroline joined, then it struck me. This was our song for cheering up. Dianne began that tradition when she moved away after Momma's death. It was a song that was needed when things felt so awful.

There we were. Three middle-aged women sitting under an oak tree humming our favorite America song. Caroline said, "This feels so good. If we did this at Dorothea Dix, the nurses would bring medicine all around. They would be sure we were having a breakdown."

The song worked to ease our anxiety. All three of the living Nash sisters began laughing. I visualized the Dix Hill nurses running toward us with three cups of water and medicine. For me, it was a belly laugh. A bending over laugh. An uncontrollable laugh with tears and everything. As we looked at each other, it kept going. Soon we were laughing just at the way each other was laughing.

It took a long time for us to stop the hysterics. I was spent. "Holy moly! I need something to eat!"

"Me too!" agreed Annie. "That was a work out! I'm starved!"

"Me three," said Caroline. "And I know just where to go. There is a diner within walking distance just down this street. And it's open in the evening.

After having chicken salad sandwiches and iced tea, we strolled back to the hospital. Annie went up to see Marie and then Caroline took her turn before visiting hours were over. I told them I would like to stay and be with Marie just as planned and said, "Annie and Caroline, you both should go get some rest. I'll walk with you outside." Standing by the door and waving goodbye I watched my sisters leave, so grateful that we had joined in strength on this day.

Caroline
Waiting for Healing

YESTERDAY AS ANNIE AND I walked out the front doors of Mary Elizabeth Hospital I saw the taxi that was to deliver me back to The Hill waiting patiently for me. I explained to Annie why I had a carriage awaiting me.

"Dr. Redmond has arranged this for me to be ready in the morning and the end of day. He told me it was going to be here whenever I wanted it. No certain time was needed. The driver's name is Buddy. He told me Dr. Redmond had been his doctor for years and now he was well enough to have his own taxi business.

"Sister, Buddy told me that I was really lucky to have him as my doc. He said, "I'll do anything for that man. When he told me about you and your family, I was ready to help. I know how it is to need to get somewhere and not havin' a way to do it."

Lucky is right.

I told Annie I wanted to go back to The Hill that night where things were settled and that I would see her in the morning. Oddly enough, I missed my own place. I never thought I'd even want to go back to the insane asylum. But it is my asylum. Yesterday had been a tiring and emotional day as we reconnected by talking, crying, laughing, and just being together. I felt like the worries I carried were a lighter load after both my sisters arrived. Once I got home, I collapsed in my bed and slept soundly.

This morning as I walked over to the place where Buddy said he would wait for me, I noticed the air was cooler and less humid.

"Good morning, Miss Nash. It is going to be a good day. Do you feel that breeze? God is breathing his love to us today. Are we going to the hospital this morning, or do you need to stop somewhere first?"

"Buddy, it will be a good day. I feel it. Please deliver me to my sisters at Mary Elizabeth Hospital."

When I rode with Buddy, I offered him a dollar, but he never took it. Today he said, "I won't take your money. Dr. Redmond pays me real well."

Larry and Annie were sitting in the lobby when I arrived. I nearly skipped over to them. They stood abruptly like they were afraid I might land on them.

"Larry, I had forgotten what you looked like. How'd you finagle your way out of Al's house? Good to see you."

Larry had a bone to pick with me. "I thank you for planning and organizing everything for Ethel, but you forgot to put me in the schedule. I've hardly seen her. I came to take her to breakfast and see what she might look like. How's that, missy?"

I giggled. "Well . . . I guess that can work." I never felt I was a power that everyone listened to. I kinda liked it. Annie seized the opportunity. "Oh good. I'll go up and relieve Ethel. She needs a good meal. She looks way too skinny these days."

Larry gave us a silent stare. Not like him to miss a reply to that.

All was settled. I found a comfortable chair and pulled out the lined paper I'd brought with me. It was time to write thank you notes to all who made this possible. First was Dr. Redmond.

It seemed like hours had passed. I went to the reception desk and asked to be allowed to visit Frank Pollard. "I don't believe Mr. Pollard has had visitors, and I would really like to see him. He is important to my family."

The reception lady allowed me up. "Sign here. He is in room 214."

I hoped that would at least get me up to the patient floors. Then I could sneak into Marie's room with Annie. I was a little scared to see Frank. I had no idea what to expect.

I quietly opened the door to room 214 and peeked in. He was still and his eyes were closed. I heard the whirr of machines next to his bed. Even though it was morning, the room was dark except for what seemed to be nightlights. As my eyes adjusted, I walked to Frank's bed. I touched his arm which was cold. Not dead cold, but needs-a-blanket cold. I pulled the covers over his arms and tucked them in a bit.

"Frank, it's me, Caroline. I just came to talk." I noticed his chest lightly rising and falling.

"You've had a tough time, but I hear you are going to make it. That's good. Ethel's been to visit and gives us reports on you. I wanted to come and verify her analysis."

I looked around the room. He had no flowers, no magazines, no sign of anyone caring for him. So sad. Just a cup of water on a table by the bed. I wondered who was supposed to drink that.

"Frank, I'm so sorry you got hurt. But I am glad you are not going to die. The Nash family needs you. And Eli needs you. He needs his daddy. Ethel, even though she might not say it, needs you too. Can I pray for you? Maybe God will be able to find you if the prays come from this room."

So Frank could hear me but not be really disturbed, I scooted the chair close to the bed and just above a whisper said the Lord's Prayer. After that I told him about everything that recently had happened with me taking a turn being the Nash sister that helped.

"Frank, I never thought I would be valuable to anyone except Joe. He often tells me he needs me. Otherwise, I am not needed a lot. My sisters don't say I am, but being a burden is clear as day when you are like me."

Let me tell you a story. I like this story because it involves you. As a kid, you were the only boy I knew that would be worth spending time with. You took time with me, as Ethel's little sister. You were so handsome and sweet. I kinda had a crush on you. Did you know that?"

Frank was still. He did not flicker his eyes or move any part of his body even the slightest bit.

"Frank, I knew it was hard for you to leave Ethel. Not because anyone told me, but I just knew. The days before Marie was born, I saw you in Ethel's bedroom at our home painting the walls two different colors—one for her and another for the baby. You went to school, worked at a job, and came over to our house to get the baby's room ready. You and Ethel had dreams for the future. I liked hearing you talk about it. People don't talk about dreams together unless they really love each other. Otherwise, what's the point?"

I sat up in the chair and did some thinking. "Frank, did you know you are gonna be a grandaddy again? Marie keeps gettin' pregnant and popping them out. This baby is a fighter. I have no doubt it could have died in the crisis of August 25th. But you did not. Marie did not. Now this baby has a responsibility to live well for this family and his or herself. It will make something of life. God will guide. And I can't wait to watch."

I stayed silent for a time. I wanted to hear a heart beat or see his eyes open. He was sleeping as soundly as any baby I have ever seen. I slouched in the chair, leaned my head back and dozed off.

People were softly talking. I woke to see two nurses and a doctor standing by Frank. I knew who was who because of the color of their uniforms. And I have lots of experience with the look of doctors and nurses. I perked right up, hoping not to have broken any rules by being there.

"Hello, doctor and nurses, I am Caroline Nash. I am a close family member to Frank. I just wanted to check on him."

A woman with blond hair tied up in a pony tail, spoke first. "And what is your relation to Mr. Pollard?"

"I'm his sister-in-law. No, not really. My niece is his daughter. It's complicated. Anyway. How is he doing? He definitely gets an A plus in sleeping."

The doctor was taking his vitals and took a moment before he spoke. "Miss Nash, this man is a miracle. He had broken bones, a punctured lung, a ruptured spleen, and a bad blow to the head. It will take a while for him to be up and around and for us to see if there is any permanent brain damage. I'm Dr. Ellis. I've met Mrs. Martin. Is she your sister?"

"Yes sir, she is. She's a strong one too because Marie Roberts in room 324 is her daughter and Frank is her first love. Oh crap, too much information. Anyway Dr. Redmond is my doctor. He said he has been in touch with you. Are you confused yet? Because if you're not, I can keep talking."

The nurses giggled. Dr. Ellis kept his composure.

"Miss Nash, thank you for visiting Mr. Pollard. From what I hear he has not had anyone visit him except Mrs. Martin. Every patient needs those around who care for them. Even when there is little response."

Relief washed over me. "Well, that's a good thing, because I have been talking a blue streak."

I glanced at my watch and realized I needed to find my sisters. I reached over to touch Frank's forehead and push his hair back. "Frank, don't you forget us.

We will be back to look in on you. Get well."

As I walked out the door, I realized once again, that I had been helpful. Frank needs visitors. I can certainly do that.

Instead of sneaking in to see Marie, I went back to the lobby. I didn't need to get caught breaking the rules.

Annie was at the public telephone in the lobby. She was talking seriously to someone. I hoped it wasn't more bad news coming from someone.

After she hung up, she came over to me and gave me a big hug. "I just talked to Jon and was able to speak to my children. They are doing just fine without me. Maybe even better than if I was home. Jon Jr told me all the things they have done since I left. It sounds like they are being spoiled. Where have you been?"

I told her about my visit with Frank. Even though I was feeling pretty proud of myself, she asked, "Are you okay? That wasn't too much on you, was it?"

"It was wonderful, Annie. People need to bring love around him so he can heal. I like doing that."

Changing the subject, I asked, "How is the place you're staying?"

"Jon made good arrangements for sure. Yellow Gables is a small tourist hotel. It's really close by. He told me last night when I called him that he booked three rooms just in case more people needed a place to stay. He told me he almost booked me into a place called Hotel Nash downtown. It would be perfect for us Nash sisters.

"When I told Ethel about that, she said, 'Wouldn't it

be cool if we had family that owned Hotel Nash? As much time as we spend in Raleigh, we need a place owned by relations where we can get discounts. Later we can drive over and introduce ourselves.'

"Speak of the devil or just our sister, here she comes."

Ethel came in the front door with a bang. Like it was her own home, she greeted the whole room yelling, "Hey y'all, it is a beautiful day!"

I waved both arms high to get her attention.

Ethel walked over to us looking radiant. The best I've seen her in a while.

To capture us in her good mood she said, "Thank you, sisters, for the great day. Annie, how was your visit with Marie?"

"Ethel, we talked non-stop. She looks good. You do too, by the way."

Ethel twirled so her skirt would fly around her. "I spent hours with Larry at breakfast and sitting outside on the bench. I feel great too. It felt like we were court'n again. Things are looking up for all of us."

Annie added to the good news. "I came down here, so Al could visit. It seems hard for him to get away from work. He and Marie are still up there together. It's been at an hour or so. I imagine he will be coming down shortly. And Caroline, I know you visited Frank. How was he?"

Ethel's face went quiet. "You did? Is he okay?"

I told them about trying to slip upstairs to see Marie and Annie together, but decided to spend time with Frank. "Ethel, I don't know how he has been when you visit, but he's just a body sleeping in the bed. He's still unconscious and hooked up to machines. I talked to him anyway. I prayed over him. It was sad to see him like that, but the alternative is much worse. I met his doctor and two nurses. They are doing the best they can for Frank. It will be a long row to hoe for him."

We all got quiet.

The day seemed to pass more quickly with Al, Larry, Annie, Ethel, and me taking turns visiting Marie and catching up with each other. Al couldn't stay long because he had to go to work, and Larry left late in the afternoon to pick up Marie's children from Barbara. That just left us sisters. Ethel seemed in better spirits after spending time with Larry today. I was glad about that. I know all this with Marie and Frank has been hard on her. And Annie was happy she got to talk with Jon and her children. As my thoughts drifted over the day, I decided, all in all, it had been a pretty good one.

Now I needed to get us organized, so I said, "It is about time for us to leave. Can I go check out your place, Annie? How about then you take me back to Dix, okay? I can be back in the morning. I'll get here by ten, Ethel, to take the next shift looking over Marie. I know you will want to stay the night again."

Annie teased me about being the new boss lady. "Do you enjoy giving orders, Caroline?"

I quickly replied, "Yep, I really do." My sisters both grinned at me.

Moving us on, Annie said, "Sounds like a good

plan, Caroline. We appreciate it. And appreciate you, Caroline." She handed us both a small piece of paper. "I want to make sure you both have this. It's the telephone number for Yellow Gables. Call me immediately if there is any news."

Before she turned to go back upstairs, I saw Ethel stop and bow her head. I overheard her say something that filled my eyes with tears.

"Dear God, please heal my Marie. She has never done anything wrong. Those little children need their momma. And, God, please let her daddy recover."

CHAPTER 10 — AUGUST 29, 1954

Caroline
Redemption

I WOKE WITH THE SUN shining on my face. I looked at my watch. Nine-thirty. Oh damn. I looked around wondering where the heck I was. I sat up to get a good look around. My brain started working. I got scared. I don't remember sleeping in a strange bedroom. Ever.

I looked over at the bedside table. There was a card there. Okay, I got it now. I am at Yellow Gables. I stayed with Annie. We bashed each other's ears until way past my bedtime. Oh yeah, Annie had said it would be too late to go back to The Hill after we talked so long, so we might as well have a slumber party. Although there was not much slumber. I have been taught all my life to *be prepared*. I had my packed bag with me. An extra set of underwear, a toothbrush, washcloth, and an extra day's worth of medicine just in case. My blue denim bag was right there on the chair.

I told Ethel last evening I would be back at Marie's room today at ten o'clock. Oh Jeez, I gotta move! And I need to call the house mother and tell her what is going on. I better find out what's going on first.

There was a knock at the door. "Yeah? Who's there?"

"Oh good, Caroline. I'm glad you're awake. It's me, Annie. Time to get up. Open the door. I have coffee and a ham biscuit."

I stepped across the room, wondering where I had gotten this sleep shirt. My head was spinning as I opened the door. "Jumpin' Jehoshaphat, Annie. I don't remember how all this happened. I must be in big trouble at home. And Ethel was expecting me . . ."

After Annie stepped in, Ethel followed. Annie attempted to calm my anxiety. "It's okay, Caroline. We got you covered. Just for a moment I took charge last night, called Dix Hill, and told them you were with us and doing fine. I said you would sleep here. I am not sure who I was talking to, but the woman asked if you had your overnight bag with your medicine. More than clean underwear, they wanted to make sure you had medicine. They told me to count your pills and describe the ones in each bottle."

Ethel piped in. "Turns out that fancy hospital arranges the taxi for you anytime day or night. And the driver knew just where Yellow Gables was. I got here about one o'clock and you were sacked out!"

Ethel looked good. She was happy and looked all cleaned up. Annie, as always, looked like she just stepped off the cover of a magazine. I grabbed my bag, removed my medicine bottles, and pulled out the pills I am supposed to take with breakfast. I downed them with my coffee and ate several bites of the biscuit.

Annie handed me a full glass of water with a lid. She knew I would need it. "Slow down, sister," she said. "We have plenty of time. Ethel has great news!"

I looked over at Ethel as I was gulping.

Ethel raised her cup of coffee in the air as a toast or something. "Marie had the baby. Or at least they took the baby out at 11:04 p.m. That's what they put on the birth certificate anyway. She and the baby are okay. Marie has a bit of pain from the surgery, but that baby girl was snuggling on her breast before I left.

"A girl? It's a girl!" I shouted jumping up and down like a teenager.

"Yep. It's a girl. A big girl. Just over eight pounds. I'm glad the doctor took it out, because I cannot imagine having something that big come from the you-know-what!"

Annie had to remind us she was the most pitiful in child birthing. "Don't forget I was carrying two at a time and pushed them out of there myself."

I looked into Annie's eyes and was surprised she could talk about that tragedy so easily. She smiled, then seem to regret letting those words come out.

Ethel patted her on the back and said to her, "Yes, you did, Annie. That was quite the accomplishment. The happiness that came from that was baby Dianne."

Each of us ate our biscuit and drank our coffee in silence. My mind was ticking off a list of things that should be done today. But I let go needing to arrange everything.

I asked my sisters what the plan was for today.

Ethel took over the conversation. "Before we get organized for the day, I want to tell you about my time with Marie last night. She and I talked a long time. Only about happy things though. We talked about how much she loved cars since before she was old enough to drive. She reminded me how ridiculous it was that I would not let her have the first car that Frank gave her. I told her I needed to break it in before she took it to State College. She said, 'You know, Momma, that was all about control over my life and not letting Frank in. You know that, right?' I tried to convince her by saying, 'Breaking in a car is important. You might drive it too fast in its first year. Even Larry says you need to be gentle with cars in the beginning.'

"Marie wasn't buying it even though she was getting pretty drowsy. I heard what sounded like a laugh. First one I'd heard since I got here. She said, 'Momma, remember it was used. A used car when Frank bought it.'

"About then a nurse, Tilly I think her name was, pulled the curtain back and poked her head in. She told me I needed to leave because Marie needed to rest to be ready to deliver that baby before long. I stayed in the chair like I was strapped to it. Marie was watching me. She tugged on my hand and said, 'Momma, don't argue. I love you.'

"Of course, I melted. I kissed her head and told her

I knew that. Then I reminded her, when it was time, to listen for the baby's breath in rhythm with hers. I told her that when I got to see her and the new baby, we could listen for all of our breaths together and hear my momma's too. I told her that her grandma would like to know this baby. It's a survivor.

"Tilly doesn't know about us, but she looked at Marie and me like she wanted to and said, 'This baby is lucky to have such a close family. We will take good care of things for now.'

"Marie's eyes were closed by then. She looked so peaceful. I put my hand on her belly and encouraged the baby to come out healthy and said that we'd help with the rest. It was so hard leaving the room.

Time seemed to drag by after that, but when one of the nurses finally came to tell me we had added a baby girl to the Nash family, a load of worries lifted, and I was full of happiness! They let me see Marie and the baby for just a few minutes, but then made me leave so they could do whatever they needed to do. Sisters, we have a new Nash baby!"

After a few quiet moments, Ethel returned to her regular self. Clearing her throat, she spit out the plan as if she had been in charge all along.

"This afternoon, all three of us are going back to the hospital to see my new grandbaby in the nursery. When I called this morning, the nurse said all three of us can see Marie at the same time, because they moved her to an obstetrics unit. I never heard of that before. But this place is known for taking care of at-risk mothers and babies differently than any other hospital. We lucked out by the ambulance bringing her here. We can bring flowers to her room and up to four family members can visit at once. Al and Larry are there now. Barbara is keeping the children. That's why I am here."

Annie continued the itinerary. "Caroline, call the house mother to prove that you are okay and that we did not kidnap you. Take a bath. Get cleaned up. After we peek at the baby and see Marie, we're going to see Al Jr, Mary, and Jimmy. They need some family around them."

Happy that these plans were getting made by my very capable sisters, I said, "I don't have Sunday visiting clothes with me. Can we swing by my house?"

Annie told us she brought enough clothes from DC to outfit us all. She left the room to go gather clothes to share.

I was glad to have some time with Ethel. I said, "I am so sad about Frank."

Ethel's good mood took a turn. I knew it would, but I had to know how she was feeling. She sat on the bed and patted it for me to sit next to her. "You know most of this, Caroline. God did not take him. And the weirdest thing happened. Right after Marie's doc had been to tell me her surgery went well your Dr. Redmond entered the room. He asked about Marie. He said he had just checked on Frank and that his latest surgery went well. The cardiologist was pleased that Frank did not have major damage to his heart. Dr. Redmond said, "Frank will have a long recovery. He will need a strong family with him like the Nash sisters. But he will make it.""

I saw a huge weight lift from Ethel's shoulders. Mine too after seeing Frank so still in his bed. "Dr. Redmond is an excellent doctor, Ethel. But more than that, he is a good man. I told Annie, but I don't think I told you, he was the one to drive me to the hospital the first day. He asked his secretary to clear his calendar that day because he needed to consult with a doctor at another hospital. He said, 'And I need Caroline to assist.' He really said that, Ethel. He thought I could assist!"

Ethel's smile was as big as a jack-o-lantern. Then she said the sweetest thing. "Not only can you assist, Caroline, you can run the whole show! You have managed things for me to help me get through this. I don't know what I would have done without you."

My reply was what I've been thinking for a time now. "Ethel, I now believe I am not a crazy, no-good sister. I am a sister that can be something good in this world. I just happen to live in an insane asylum."

Ethel grabbed me and gave me a big hug. "Yes, you can, Caroline. Yes, you can. You are a Nash sister."

I know I will always remember these days as the best ones in my life. It is odd because they are also terrible days for our family. I have had many good days in my life, but I've never felt important before.

Marie
Back to Normal

IT HAS BEEN OVER A month since bringing Emma Lou home from the hospital. She came home with me to meet her brothers and sister five days after her birth day on August 28th. The time has flown by, but in a normal way. Al Jr and Mary are at school every day. Jimmy is around being helpful. About a week after Emma Lou and I came home, he decided he wanted to wear "boy boy pants." I think he noticed baby girl was wearing diapers, and he didn't want to be a baby anymore. So, we gave it a try. We took off the diaper and just used short pants. I didn't want to buy any underwear yet, because this might not work. One good thing about Jimmy's quirky personality is he doesn't like having wet pants. Within two weeks he had trained himself to go to the toilet. For nighttime though, Al Jr demanded he use a diaper because they sleep in the same bed.

Al Jr is seven and adores "his baby." Mary is

nearly six and jealous of the sister. I have to watch Mary closely because there is a tiny bit of meanness in that child. Momma said Mary takes after her. Geez that makes me worry about the future.

Emma Lou is a sweet, easy baby. She sleeps a lot, is easily soothed, and loves her daddy. Al didn't have much to do with the others when they were little. He said he likes children who can talk to him. But Emma Lou melted his heart right away. He stops reading the paper or gets up from his chair when she murmurs. Momma says this is how Frank was with me. "Absolutely infatuated," she said.

Momma has been staying at a tourist home nearby. Those are rented week by week and cost less than a motel. Annie returned to DC two weeks after Emma Lou was born. The Yellow Gables was close to the hospital but not close to my home. Momma got a recommendation from the Yellow Gables' owner about a place on the west side of downtown. That's how she and Larry ended up in the Lewis house. Caroline moved back to "The Hill," as she now calls it. She was able to move into a smaller cottage on campus. Only two bedrooms. She says it feels like how normal people live.

I'm secretly happy that Momma and Larry/Dad have put off their move to Surf City on Topsail Island. I know Larry/Dad is disappointed, but he has been so good about it. He and Suzy are running The Kooler business in Burlington together while Momma is in Raleigh with me. I called him yesterday to thank him for the umpteenth time for all his help with me and my children. And for him driving back and forth when he comes to see Momma.

"Marie darlin', you being well and the children gettin' over this trauma is all that matters right now. I'm still packing boxes to move someday. Maybe before the end of the year. Don't you worry about me and Ethel. I think some marriages do better when there is sometimes a little space. Don't tell your momma I said that."

I could feel his grin coming through the telephone. "Dad, you are the best."

It's Sunday tomorrow, and I wanted to start back going to church with the children. Al cares nothing about church and only goes with us on holidays. But I need that formal connection to God. I can't remember when Al Jr and Mary last went to Sunday school. It was time.

When I told Al my plan, he was not too happy. "Al, I need to get back to church regularly. The older children need it too. I know you don't like going. We've talked about that hundreds of times, but I want to go. You can keep Jimmy and Emma Lou."

"Naw, I can't, Marie. I got things I need to do. Anyway, I haven't kept Emma Lou by myself yet. It's too soon. Call Ethel and see if she can come get them."

I was furious. But getting mad never worked with Al. I sat next to Al on the sofa. "Al, these children are ours. They need time with their daddy. You will be fine with Emma Lou. All you need to do is hold her or walk around with her. I'll get her fed and diapered before I leave for church. Jimmy will be over the moon about spending time with his daddy. Besides, Momma is coming with me to church. There is a guest pastor tomorrow that I want her to hear. He grew up in the area near Momma's homeplace. She wants to meet him and talk about home."

"Shit, woman," he said and went out the back door. I imagine he was going to have a cigarette.

That wasn't a yes. But it's the closest I will get. We did not speak of it again.

The next morning, I got Emma Lou fed, bathed, and into her cutest dress. She smelled like sweetness. How could he resist? I told Jimmy he was going to stay with Daddy and Emma Lou this morning. "Jimmy, Grandma, Mary, little Al, and I are going to church this morning. We are going to say prayers to keep our family well." I showed Jimmy the universal symbol for praying. Two palms meeting together with fingertips under my chin.

Jimmy understood more of what was happening than I thought. He raised his hands up to reach me and said, "Bye bye, Momma." He mimicked my prayer sign.

As she stepped in the front door, Momma said to Al, "Hey y'all! I'm here to help the children get dressed. They haven't been to church in so long, they probably forgot how to clean up for God."

Al just grunted.

Then Momma responded with her usual sarcasm. "Well, hello to you too, young man! Yes, I am glad to see you!"

He growled out a response. "Yeah, thanks for taking Marie away from her children."

Momma walked over to him and mockingly kissed him on his head. "And thank you for watching your own kids, Albert."

She knew how to get his goat. She took quick steps to the children's room and shouted, "Grandma's here! Let me help you get ready for God."

I had been listening from the hallway hoping Al didn't bust a gasket at being called Albert. I whispered emphatically, "Momma, hush. Let's just do this." And in a louder tone I said, "Come, children, show your grandma how sharp you look!"

Al Jr has the temperament of his daddy sometimes. "Grandma, why do we have to dress different for God. I know he's around all the time. Nobody's fooling him."

Both Momma and I hid our chuckle.

Momma pulled herself together and said, "Yeah, you are right, little Al, but we have to show others we can dress up for church. People are expecting that. Wowie, don't we look fantastic today!"

We headed out the front door. I bent down and kissed Emma Lou in her daddy's arms and said to Jimmy, "You be a good boy. Help your daddy with the baby girl!"

He blew us a kiss. "Bye bye, Momma! Bye bye, Grandma!"

As the children climbed into the back seat of the car, Barbara Liberman and her children were heading toward their car. Mary yelled, "Hey y'all! Do you want to come to church with us?"

Barbara waved. "We aren't going to church today. We go on Saturday. We're heading downtown for haircuts. We'll see you when you get back. Y'all look pretty as a picture!"

I looked at Momma with that look she taught me how to do. It said *don't say a word.* She recognized it and kept quiet. I knew what she was thinking would come out later.

Pulling up to the church with Momma and my two children gave me great pride. I wanted to be the kind of family that Momma and all my daddies had together. Church was important. It was not a matter of liking it or not. It was just what we did. It was where we thought about being good people. Where we learned to live a life of service to others and prayed for those who had less. It was in church where I first learned about fairness and equality and to look for the good in the world. I want that for my children. And someday, Al might come with us. He needs God in his life. He just doesn't know it yet.

After the service, we were greeted outside by many people. Even some we did not know, but they evidently knew us. Several of the neighbors and their children came over to say hello.

"Marie, you look quite well."

"I am glad to see you up and about. How is the baby?"

"Children, you look quite dashing! Glad to see you at church!"

"Marie, this must be your mother. You look like sisters!"

Momma smiled. Her cheeks turned pink.

As the crowd began to clear out, a young man and woman came over to us. I did not recognize them, but it seemed they knew us. Oddly enough, little Al knew the young man. With a grown-up greeting, Al put out his hand to shake hands with the man. "Hello, Mr. William. It's good to see you. Momma, this is the man that took you to the hospital."

I was stunned. So was Momma. She asked to understand. "Mr. William, is it? How does our boy know you?"

Mary spoke up, "I know him too, Grandma. When Momma almost died, Mr. William came and kept her alive. He said he would take care of you, Momma. And he did."

Al Jr then spoke to him—boy to man. "Mr. William, doesn't my momma look terrific. She got well. And she brought my baby sister, Emma Lou, home from the hospital!"

Momma stepped over to William and put her arms around his shoulders. I'd never see her hug a stranger before. I heard her say, "Thank God for you, young man."

"I am sorry I don't remember you, Mr. William. I am thankful for you."

He responded, "And I am thankful to see you looking so well, Mrs. Roberts. And the baby? Is she doing well?"

"She is a beautiful, sweet, perfect baby girl. Thanks to you and the doctors at Mary Elizabeth Hospital."

William placed his arm around the woman who

was standing beside him and brought her into our circle. "Mrs. Roberts, this is my wife, Helen. Helen, this is Mrs. Roberts."

Looking at my momma he said, "I am sorry I don't know your name, but you must be related. You favor Mrs. Roberts. It is good to meet you. This is my wife, Helen."

Momma stood a little taller and smiled. "I'd like to say I'm her sister, but I'm actually Marie's mother. It is good to meet you both."

Mary and Al Jr stood closer to the couple in a way that showed ownership. Mary looked admiringly at Helen. Helen kneeled down and began a conversation with her. I couldn't hear what was being said, but I could tell the children liked her.

William began a conversation with Momma and me. "As a medic, I don't often know how the patients do after I treat them. It is wonderful to see you again, Mrs. Roberts."

"Please call me Marie," I said.

And Momma chimed in, still feeling flattered, "And call me Ethel."

William smiled and nodded at Momma. "Marie, do you know how the man driving the car is doing? It was a terrible accident, and I never was able to follow-up."

I looked at Momma wondering which way to steer this conversation.

Momma took over. "William, that man is Marie's father. He was coming to see Marie and took the curve way too fast. Although he doesn't remember anything about that day, we have pieced it all together with the doctors and neighbors. Frank Pollard is his name. He is better and back home in Virginia with his wife and little boy. We are so glad that we didn't lose him. That wreck could've killed him."

I put my hand on Momma's arm to signal her to stop talking. She got it. "Oh, I am talking your ears off. There is so much to say about Frank, Marie, and young men like you who save lives. Maybe someday we can meet again and learn more about each other."

To draw this to a close, I reached out to both William and Helen. "We just want you to know how important you are in this world. Please never forget that. I owe you such a debt. I am sure there are many others that do also. I hope we will see you often here at church."

Helen put her hand over mine and found the most generous words. "Marie, there is a reason William was there that day. He could have answered a call somewhere else. But it was meant for him to be there. With you. William's patients do not always present him this kind of gift. Sadly, so often the people he meets in his job get to him too late. You are destined to do great things in your life. And so is your baby girl. I just know it. We would very much like to stay in touch."

As they both turned to leave, I found myself weeping, but called out, "William, I will try to live up to this miracle."

He looked back at me and nodded. "I am sure you will, Marie."

Momma wrapped her arm around my shoulders and turned me toward the car. "Come on, everyone. Let's get back home. I am starving."

CHAPTER 12 — OCTOBER 13, 1954

Ethel
Hazel

LARRY IS SNORING LIKE A bull. I can't sleep, but that's not why. I am used to the snoring. The trick is to get to sleep before he does. Then I'm not bothered.

The air is hot and smells sweaty tonight. Both of us are laying in the bed with nothing but a sheet over us. The windows are open with the venetian blinds pulled all the way up. We are hoping for a breeze. The curtains are not moving. Nothing is. The night is still for a reason. It knows something's coming, but it does not want us to know.

For the last several days, the television in the main room of the boarding house has been announcing Hurricane Hazel. It's supposed to be a big one. Four days ago they said it was a Category 4 and coming right for the coast of North and South Carolina. We know about hurricanes. They come through every year. Every now and then, they tear everything up in their path.

We had Hurricane Carol at the end of August. It stayed over the ocean and just brushed up against our Outer Banks while heading north to drop all the rain it could make. I am glad Marie was in the hospital then. That building was good and strong. She hardly felt it. She kept that grandbaby of mine in her bed all night. Annie, Larry, and I stayed up together that night at the Yellow Gables. Caroline was back at her home. The whole family was hunkered down.

Then Hurricane Edna came two weeks later, and she was fierce. Edna was a traveler. She did damage all the way up to the Northeast. Since Carol had not been so bad, we didn't worry too much about Edna. It looked like she was on the same path as Carol. But she was different. Edna brought heavy rain and winds that pushed the ocean onto land all the way up to the top of the United States into Maine. The news said New York got more rain than they had seen in forty-five years. It was all terrifying.

Now they are saying Hurricane Hazel is aiming right for the coast of North Carolina. Just thinking about my family made the hair on my arms stand up.

I was glad Annie had gone back and was settled in at home in DC. Jon said before Hurricane Edna arrived, the government demanded that people take cover. Annie had told me on the telephone how stupid that was. "For one thing, Ethel, people do take cover. They have some sense. Another thing is, if the hurricane is bad enough, it won't matter. Homes will be flooded or blown over."

"Annie, I think Hazel is going to be worse. People

haven't cleaned up from the other two. Where are y'all going? I love your house on the hill in Arlington, but how much more can it take?"

To ease my fear, she told me their plans. "We are going to the Pentagon to stay with Jon in his office. It will be a family camping trip. We are taking sleeping bags, pillows, snacks, flashlights, and games. We'll be fine. That building is a solid block."

Helping me check off the family list, Annie asked, "Has Caroline said what preparation the Dix campus is making for the residents?"

"Caroline said as many of the residents as they can fit are going to stay in the Dorothea Dix hospital. She's been helping make rounds in her car to carry people's stuff over there. Annie, this is exactly what she said, 'We'll be packed like sardines, and it will probably stink like that after a night there. I'll bet there's gonna be pills by the bucket for all those crazy people head-to-head, butt-to-butt.'"

The picture of that was too much. Annie and I both giggled. Larry could hear the conversation. He pinched his nose with his thumb and pointer finger and in a big voice so Annie could hear, said, "**Pee U!**"

He can be disgusting. But we still laugh.

After pulling myself together, I ran the list of family members in my head. I wanted to make sure they were getting ready. "How about Lelia? What will her family do?"

Annie said, "Ethel, like you say, we know how to deal with this in the South. It's an every year thing. Lelia and her family are heading to West Virginia.

They have cousins and a big extended family there. Leila said there are more Arringtons in West Virginia than anywhere on earth. They will be far enough inland that I think they will be okay."

"I checked in with Elizabeth and Frank. When she answers the telephone, she won't let me speak to him. It was a quick conversation about them going to visit her family in Philadelphia. I didn't say this to her, Annie, but I think they are not going far enough. I guess Frank knows what he is doing."

To wrap it all up, I reminded Annie, "As for us, we will have a full house 200 miles west in Burlington. Larry and me are heading out today. Marie and the kids are coming too. Larry thinks he can talk Al into going with us, but I'm not sure. I told Marie she can't hang back because Al's stubborn. Suzy's there and asked if Francie could stay with us. Of course she can if she wants to. Suzy said Francie's mother doesn't believe anything special needs to be done."

"Ethel, please keep yourself safe. The Nash sisters have a lot more living to do. This year has been too scary already. We will talk on the other side of this. Kiss kiss!"

Larry went to talk to Mrs. Lewis about our plans. He was figuring he could get a discount on the room while we were gone, so we'd have a place to come back to. Most people in the South accommodate. But Mrs. Lewis was from Long Island, NY. She had a different thought.

"Mr. Martin, I can't do that. We might have people coming in to move away from the coast. I need to be able to rent your room. You can pay for the room, and I will hold it for you. But otherwise, no go."

I had everything packed up when he came back to the room. "She said no go, Ethel. We either pay and have a room or don't pay and have to find a new place when we come back. Whatcha wanna do?"

When I am frustrated, I look for a reason people are like they are. "Northerners! I guess we just go. I ain't paying for something that might get blown away by Hazel."

After the car was packed, we returned the key, and I silently gave her a fist in the air.

We went to Marie's and expected another fight on our hands about Al not wanting to leave. Larry said, "Let me go in first, Ethel. You stay out here. I'm gonna convince Al that a husband has to go with his wife and kids to keep them safe."

"Good luck with that."

I walked to the edge of the street where Frank wrecked his car. The tree that he hit had been cut down. It was a big oak with wide branches that covered two yards. The neighbors brought their saws and took it down branch by branch. The large sawed-off stump will be a lifetime memory of the place where my first boyfriend was nearly killed. It felt eerie. I'll be glad when Al and Marie get their own house and won't have to see this.

I heard the screen door close and saw Marie carrying two big suitcases. "I know, Momma, it's hard, isn't it? I try to ignore it every time I'm out here. I want to go see him. Will you go visit him later this year? Maybe near Christmas?"

I grabbed one of her bags to put in their car. "Yeah,

we can do that. But I want to make sure the witch he married is not around."

"Not sure that will happen if we want to see Eli."

Larry came out of the house carrying bags, and Al was behind him with the children in tow. "Ethel, let's take Al Jr in our car. Al is filling up theirs with tools. He says he'll need them to fix things after the storm comes through. I told him we had tools. But he wanted to bring his own tools since we are on the run to Burlington to stay safe from Hazel."

I looked over at Marie and smiled. Marie raised her shoulders a bit to tell me this was a surprise to her. Larry is good at talking men into doing the right thing.

We drove for the first hour and barely made it out of Raleigh. I thought going early would get us where we needed to be before others figured it would be smart to head west. Traffic was moving at a snail's pace. Larry was leading our two-car caravan. Looking at the side mirror, I could see Al's car behind us. After we got through Durham, Al began turning his headlights on and off, then put his turn signal on.

Larry's eyes were on the rearview mirror, "Ethel, we need to pull over. Al's trying to signal something. He pulled off at the next road and parked on the side. Al did the same. Both men got out and stood on the field side of the car. They talked for a few minutes. When Larry walked back to the car, it seemed everything was okay.

As Larry got back in the car, Al Jr asked, "Is everything okay, Grandpa? How's baby Emma doing being in the car for so long?"

"Everything is fine, Al. The kids in that car have been sleeping the whole time so far. Your papa just decided we should find the nearest filling station and get the cars filled up. It would be a good idea to have a full tank before the storm comes. So that is what we are going to do."

Before he pulled the car around, Larry leaned over to me and spoke quietly, "Al said we should listen to the radio. He heard Hazel is real close to the North Carolina coast, and the governor said everyone should get to a secure place before midnight. He was asking if I knew of a place closer than Burlington to stay."

My jaw tightened. I gripped my hands tight. "We could find a motel, but everyone on the road would want to do that too. Let's keep moving. Suzy is waiting for us."

Larry looked back at little Al. He was slumped in the back seat reading a book. He didn't seem to be worried. "That's what I told Al. Pull out the map and make sure there's not a better way to get home. We know Route 70 like the palm of our hand, but we're in a bottle-neck going this way."

I spoke to Al Jr, "Do you need to pee before we get back on the road? Here's as good a place as any. We can just open the car doors to give you some privacy."

He looked at me in astonishment. "You mean just out in the open? Jeez! No, Grandma, I don't need to go that bad."

After turning around, we joined the long line of cars going west. I opened the map all the way to see the smaller roads heading out that way. "Larry, the reason we always take Route 70 is there is no better way. We can go way north on 86, but we'd need to come back south on 49 to get home. The other way would be to go south and drive parallel to 70 on route 54. We could go one of those ways, but we'd need to get back on 70 to get us home. I doubt any of those roads will be any better, and they are further in miles."

Larry agreed. "Let's just stick with what we know. There are stations in Hillsborough. We'll get fuel and use the toilet there."

All I could do was just stare at the sky. There were clouds behind us that I could see in the side view mirror. It was still looking clear ahead of us. I turned on the radio but kept the volume low enough so only Larry and I could hear it. It's a good thing we don't have a fancy car like Annie's with speakers in the back seat. I didn't want to scare little Al. Turning the dial on the radio didn't give much information. I could only pick up a few stations as the needle moved up and down the AM dial. I heard only music. There were no news broadcasts. Strange.

I picked a radio station that was playing big band and polka music. "Larry, if we weren't sitting in this traffic, you wouldn't know a deadly hurricane was riding our tail from the Bahamas."

"Yes, ma'am. It is the strangest thing. It's like the hurricane isn't real, and we've all been duped into thinking it is. The Esso filling station is just a few miles up. I'll be glad to get there and put my feet on the ground."

From the backseat Al Jr blurted out, "And I can use a real toilet! Can I get a Moon Pie, Grandpa?"

"Heck yeah! I think I'm gonna get one too," said Larry.

I joined in, "And I want a Pepsi and a pack of peanuts!"

Little Al leaned forward so he could see the dashboard. "Grandpa, point out the miles we are going so I can count them off."

Larry pointed to the odometer. "There it is, but it's moving as slow as molasses in winter. How 'bout you look out the window and count the telephone poles we pass. Grandma can tell you when we turn a mile here. Then you will know how many poles make a mile."

I smiled and touched Larry's arm with my elbow. "Okay! Here we go, little man. I'll tell you when to start. Here we go, the next number is starting to roll over. Wait, wait . . . okay! Start counting!"

Counting out loud, when he got to sixteen poles I yelled "Stop! That's one mile." Little Al was quite proud of himself. For the next half hour, he was letting us know when we had been another mile.

Larry put on his turn signal and pulled into the line that was going to the Esso filling station.

"Holy moly! Lines everywhere," I declared. Looking at my watch, I realized it was nearly dinnertime.

My stomach began to rumble. "Larry, when we get there, let's pull out the picnic basket and eat a sandwich. We can have Moon Pies and Pepsi on the side. How does that sound, little Al?"

"Good plan, Grandma. I'm hungry for a double baloney sandwich!"

It took another thirty minutes to get to the fuel pumps. As Larry pulled up to the pump, Al Jr and I jumped out to run to the bathrooms. The rest of the family was a few cars behind us. I looked back and could see their car doors open. Marie, Mary, and Jimmy piled out. They had the same idea I did.

I waited for Marie to catch up to us. "I am so tired of sitting I could scream. Most of all we need the facilities. How's it going back there?"

Marie looked exhausted. "Momma, the baby has been crying off and on the last hour. I've been holding, singing, and feeding her, but she doesn't like this any more than I do. Jimmy's aggravating his sister every minute. Mary is about to pound her little brother. We have run out of car games. Al is angry about all of this. Are y'all having fun?"

I laughed out loud. "I don't think fun and a hurricane run go together."

After we all had been to the bathroom, I pointed to a picnic table and told Al Jr to hold it for us. He and Mary took it seriously and plopped down on the benches. Jimmy came with me to the car to unload the cooler. The men finally got their gas tanks topped off and pulled the cars out of line to park near us.

I made sandwiches for everyone. Marie walked around with Emma Lou, and the men complained together about the traffic and stupid drivers.

We all ate like we hadn't had a meal in days. I did it standing up so my behind could get a standing ovation. Larry brought out Moon Pies for everyone. The children squealed.

After all the chocolate faces were wiped, Marie said, "We're going to get some exercise. Let's run some races, do some jumping jacks, and play tag. Which are we gonna do first?"

After the hour break, we packed up, organized who was riding in which car, and hit the road again. Mary and Jimmy came with us. "Al Jr, you need to ride in the other car to help your momma with the baby. She can ride in the back seat with you and you can get some training to be a babysitter."

He liked the idea. "A babysitter? Sit on a baby? That is silly, Grandma! But I can play with her."

We were less than forty-five minutes away from home on a good day. I figured it might be way past bedtime before we got there tonight. I had arranged sleeping areas in the back for Mary and Jimmy. One on the floor, and one on the seat. They had books, toys, and baby dolls to keep them busy until it got dark. I hoped they would sleep.

Chapter 13 — October 14, 1954

Suzy
Shedding a Light

MOMMA, MY SISTER, AND ALL the children got to Burlington a little after midnight on the day Hurricane Hazel hit our state. According to the radio reports, it was heading inland rather than just skirting up the coast. That wasn't good news. We thought being west of Raleigh would be safe enough.

When daylight came, Larry and Al worked hours boarding up windows, cutting limbs away from the house, and putting anything that could blow around in the storage building behind the house. That's where Momma had an inventory of new washing machines. She bought them cheap and was ready to sell at a profit when people changed their mind about sending out their dirty laundry. There were fifteen machines out there because right now people had no desire to wash, dry, and fold their own clothes.

The funny thing is, women were bringing me

clothes to do when a gigantic hurricane was heading our way. Go figure.

I was complaining to Momma about it, "People get stupid at times like this. I don't want to be responsible for their wardrobe of fancy clothes. Do we have to take them?"

Momma was always thinking profit. "Here's the deal, Suzy. We tell them we have to charge them up front and add in an extra fee for storage. Be sure to tell them we are not responsible for damage to their attire in a natural disaster. If they still want to leave laundry with us, there's no skin off our nose."

Momma's a smart woman. I learn about business from her every day. Thinking off the top of my head about a new scheme is not something I'm good at. I have to plan things out and talk to family before I change things. It's gonna be hard when she and Larry move to Topsail Island. Whatever happens with Hazel might change their decision to move and my life plan.

I might start that conversation tonight. An impending storm could make my revelation seem small.

Francie was helping me prepare dinner for an army. Everyone else was busy being mothers or storm preparers. Since she doesn't like to choose the food that gets put together in a meal, Francie is the chopper. We were making spaghetti because we had ground beef and that meal goes a long way. Turns out Marie's six- and seven-year-old kids have some experience helping in the kitchen. I pulled two chairs up to the counter and stove for them. I stood right next to them.

Al Jr's job was stirring the beef as it was cooking.

Mary was spreading the bread with butter. "Are we gonna cook the bread, Suzy?"

Like Momma, I let the children help, but there are always rules that need to be enforced. "We sure are, Mary. But I need to do the oven work. It can burn a little girl."

After the buttering was finished, Mary got preoccupied with Francie. "You're pretty. I like your red hair. Who's your momma? Do you have a daddy?"

I looked over at Francie to see how she would handle this. There are no small ones in her family.

Francie sent a small smile to me, then said to Mary, "Well, thank you, Mary. I think you are pretty too. My red hair came from my father. He is not around anymore, but I've seen pictures of him. My momma's name is Martha. She lives not far from here. I stay with her, when I am not hanging out with Suzy."

Al Jr was curious too. "Do you have a boyfriend? Or a husband?"

I stopped what I was doing and stared at Francie. The answer to this question could be dangerous. I hoped Francie would get this right. She stepped over to the stove and stood next to Al Jr. She bent down to meet him face to face.

I could tell Francie was measuring her words. "Al Jr, that is a complicated question for me. I am only twenty-two years old. I think I am too young to be married. Boyfriend? Well . . . I once had a boyfriend, but we broke up. We didn't get along. Now my best friend in the world is a girl, your aunt Suzy. Does that make sense?"

Francie looked over at me. I could have just hugged her. She handled that wonderfully.

Mary piped in. "My best friend is a girl too. I don't think a best friend can be a boy. Boys are stupid."

"Watch it, Mary!" argued Al Jr. "I'm a boy! Momma said boys are super cool to have around. You'll see that someday."

Francie, Mary, and I ended up giggling. Al Jr jumped down from the chair and stomped out of the room.

Mary thought that was the proof we needed. "See what I mean? Boys are stupid."

After supper and when the kids were tucked in, all six of us adults were squeezed around the small kitchen table. Momma got up to turn on the stove for coffee.

"Ethel, no coffee for me. I need to hit the sack and let my beat-up body recover from the workout Al put me through."

Al, who doesn't say much, needed to dispute that. "You and I did the same amount of work. It's just that you're an old man. I'm just trying to keep you in shape."

Larry let out a guffaw, crooked both arms in the air at shoulder level. He made his muscles bulge. "Man, I am only nine years older than you. This body's in great shape. Let's see how yours holds up nine years from now in 1963!"

Al intended to move the discussion outside. "Momma Ethel, you got something stronger than coffee? Larry and I should move this outside and let him complain about being old."

Momma held out a bottle of Jack Daniels to Larry and whispered, "Be easy on that body, Larry." He kissed her on the cheek.

I love my momma and daddy Larry. They are good to each other.

The screen door slammed. Then it was only us four women at the table. Marie went to close the back door behind them.

Emma Lou was sleeping soundly on a pallet on the floor. It was the first time all day I saw Marie without the baby attached to her. My heart was feeling heavy at the thought of loving someone so much you would have babies with him.

Marie was searching cabinets for something. "Momma, where is that bottle of red wine I saw you bring out of the suitcase? The women need something too."

Momma went to the back room to find it.

Marie looked over at Francie, "Are you old enough to drink? You don't come from a teetotaling family, do you?"

Both Francie and I grinned. I spoke for us. "Yeah, sister, we are both old enough and her momma drinks plenty. Yes, we'll have a glass or two."

Momma came back into the kitchen being careful not to trip on the step up. "Did somebody say a drink or two?" She was waving two bottles high above her head.

Marie grabbed short glasses from the cupboard and, like Momma, raised them in the air. She copied me and let out a hoot, "Fill 'er up!"

We sat down together just like we have all our

lives, ready for playing cards or just deep discussions. Marie on my right and Momma in her seat at the end of the table. I gently grabbed Francie's arm and said, "Francie, sit right here by me."

I got things started. "Momma, are you and Larry still moving to the coast? There is no telling how damaged it will be after the storm."

Momma finished the rest of what was in her glass in one swallow. "Larry and I have talked about it. I just don't know. We have money sunk into a building in Surf City. We're kinda stuck. It would be perfect for a two-bedroom house and the business. It will need work, but it's Larry's dream. I guess it's mine too. I think we just go down with the idea of living there and decide about opening a business after the new year. But you know what? I get all weepy about not being near either of my daughters and my present and future grandchildren."

Marie grabbed the bottle and refilled glasses all around. "I've been thinking about that too. With Suzy in Burlington and you in Surf City, I'm right smack dab in the middle. My house can be the new monthly Sunday dinner place. And in the summer, me and the kids will come stay with you at the beach. It would be so cool for the children to grow up with summers at the beach with Grandma and Grandpa! Suzy, as soon as you start your family, the cousins can grow up together down there. Beach kids forever!"

Momma added with a two-glasses-down slur, "Yeah, when you gonna start a family! I need more grandbabies! Francie, can't you help her find a man?"

I froze. I was barely breathing. My hand, under the table, searched for Francie's hand. Neither of us said a word.

Marie came to the rescue. "Oh God, Suzy. I'm sorry. I know we need to give you some time. After all, there are not many marrying kind of people in Burlington. Just forget we said that."

Francie got up from the table. "Ladies, if you don't mind, I need to go home. Hazel might come tomorrow, and I need to be with my mother. You all have lots of family matters to discuss."

Momma stood, or tried to stand. "Francie, that was an odd moment. We do that all the time. But you don't have to go. Maybe we need your perspective on this."

I ignored Momma and walked Francie out. The men were smoking cigars and telling tales about hurricanes.

As we walked by them, Francie said, "Goodnight, gentlemen. I hope Hazel is gentle."

I opened the car door for her and said, "I'm sorry too, Francie. I need to talk to them about this. But you don't have to be in the room. Will I see you tomorrow?"

"Suzy, we'll talk soon. Maybe they're right. You need a family."

As she drove off, I wondered if it was Hazel or Francie that would alter my life plan.

Building up my courage to finish this discussion, I walked back in the house. Momma was drinking water from her glass. Marie must have cut her off.

Sitting down at the table, I pulled my back straight and placed my hands on the table. I looked right at

Momma. "I feel lonely most of the time, Momma. But I am not helpless. I have always been able to do what I need to with school and the business. I don't need a man to get through life. I have seen good marriages. Momma Dianne and Papa Joe were perfect for each other. Frank, George, and Larry have added something to your life. But it didn't take a marriage license to do that."

Since they were still listening, I continued. "Marie, did you get married because that was the only way you and Al could be together? I don't think so. In fact, there was a reason you really didn't want family to know you were getting married."

Marie interrupted, "Suzy, I got married because I wanted a partner in raising a family. I know you didn't like Al, but he is a good provider. If I want children, I need a provider. Al is kind—most of the time. I am sure he loves me."

"What are you saying, Suzy?" asked Momma.

I let it out. "I don't want to marry a man. If I get a partner like you two have, it will be a woman. Women anticipate what is needed to be done. I've never had to make a To Do list for girls I knew in school. Great ideas come from discussions woman to woman. Take Francie for instance. She is kind and caring like no man I have ever known."

Momma smacked her hand on the table. "Stop, Suzy! Are you saying you like women in the way you are supposed to like men? What makes you say that? You can't be one of *those* people! That is not normal!"

The whole time I was talking, Marie was silent. I looked over at her to see if she could help me explain this to Momma. She still said nothing.

Momma kept going. Maybe it was better for her to get it all said. "We were raised by good Christian people, Suzy. Generations of them! We know better than to be tempted by wickedness. Remember what the church teaches? God created a man in his image and a female for the male. Something like that anyway. A man leaves his father and his mother and goes to a wife. Man and woman are to become one. That is the way families are made, Suzy!"

"Don't make out like I am a sinner, Momma!" Now my voice was raised as loud as hers "Preachers judge people and make them feel like they will lose their soul and go to hell if they do not do right. What is right, Momma? You told me that Jesus was a good kind man. He was a helper to all. All, Momma. All people! That is what I believe in. If you profess to be Christian, Jew, Catholic, or any other kind of religion, you must be good to all people. Respect all people! Do you believe that, Momma?"

Marie finally spoke, but in a calm voice. She looked at Momma and put one hand gently on my arm. "This is a lot to absorb. Momma, you have expectations for us. Heck, society has expectations for women in general. Suzy, you are a good person. The best sister I could ever want. And Momma, before hearing this tonight, you know she is the best daughter you could have—except for me of course." Marie giggled. But no one else saw the humor.

"Momma, is there anything about Suzy you do not love? Any piece of her that shames you?"

Momma squinched her eyebrows together and looked at Marie like she had lost her mind. "Marie, that is crazy talk. Suzy, of course I love you with all my heart. You have never disappointed me. But this . . ."

Marie said all the things I could not. And I could tell it made Momma feel bad.

"Momma, I don't understand this either, but we have to think of it as who Suzy is, not as a decision she has made to bring hurt to you or anyone. We have an amazing family. You and your sisters have taught us all how to accept and love who we are. Aunt Caroline is the greatest example of that. She has challenges. She has done some scary things. And she has worked hard to get better. None of our family judged her. Caroline is someone with mental illness. You could say she is not normal. But no one in the Nash family would ever say she was wrong for being who she is. I have come to believe that people who love others of the same sex are not wrong. They are just built that way. They are not trying to sin; they are being true to themselves."

It was a lovely speech, but I took offense at one thing. "Marie, my situation is not completely the same as Aunt Caroline. This is not a mental illness. It is an understanding of how I'm made."

Marie squeezed my hand and said, "Oh crap, Suzy. No. I didn't mean it to come out that way. I do not believe that men wanting to love men or women loving women is an illness."

All got quiet. Then the doorknob turned and the door was pushed open wide. The men stumbled inside.

Al announced, "It's starting to rain out there."

I stiffened. I was not ready to talk about this in front of them. Evidently neither was Momma.

She stood and took control. "Yep. Good timing, guys. Let's get to bed. We have to hunker down for Hazel. The children are asleep in the Suzy's double bed. Us womenfolk are gonna pile in the second bedroom with Emma Lou's bassinet. And you men will crash on the floor in the hallway. Nobody sleeps near windows. Y'all go ahead. I'll clean up here. I don't want the kitchen to be a mess when our hurricane visitor comes."

We all laughed at how ridiculous that was.

Marie headed out of the room with the men. I stayed to help Momma was the dishes. We didn't speak. We just worked together. About an hour later, we heard the wind whipping up outside and the rain coming down hard. I looked at Momma with a look a fear.

"Little girl, we are gonna be all right. In all ways, we are gonna be fine."

She embraced me with softness and warmth.

CHAPTER 14

Nash Round-Robin Letters

Burlington Family Is Okay!
Tuesday, October 19, 1954

Dear sisters and our next generation,

As soon as the sun began to shine, I peeked out the window. The sky was clear. Hazel had come and gone. Larry and I walked to town that day to see what was happening. Seeing the results of the rain and wind was upsetting. All the merchants downtown were cleaning up and clearing out.

Larry visited the grocery store, and I walked to the post office. It was open. The clerk was mopping up water and putting things in the sun to dry. I asked whether I could send and get letters. He told me they were mailing out and some were coming in. He said they had received several boxes of mail from Raleigh yesterday, and they would be sending some out as soon as the trucks could get through. He said they wouldn't be delivering to houses until everyone was back at work. That made sense. Their people needed to take care of their houses too. He really didn't know much more since telephone lines were down and so were power lines meaning none of us had radio news either. He said he had heard some post offices were severely damaged. I'm sure the postmasters will do the best they can to get the mail moving again.

Larry met me at the house an hour later with bags full of food. He said the grocery store's glass windows were blown out, and there was no electricity. The few people who were there looking around were told to buy what they could before it spoiled. Larry asked the manager if he could help, and the manager handed him a mop. He helped push the water out the front door. Neighbors brought out boxes of food to the sidewalk. Larry said it began to look like the general store from when he was a kid. Most of the food was wet but okay to eat, so he did bring some home. He said, "Like you always say, Ethel, there is a piece of happiness in the sadness."

I took the bags from him, kissed his cheek, and told him he was a good man.

After unpacking everything we had, Suzy and I began to plan the meals by first using the quickest to spoil and what could be eaten without a stove. Even the city water was out, so we couldn't wash the stuff, but we had food for all of us for the next few days, and I figured our food planning would work pretty good.

I knew it would be a while longer before we could get on the telephone, so when things settled down a little, I dusted off the best way to tell each other what was going on, and here I am typing this letter. A new Nash Round-Robin Letter. We haven't done this for a long time because we talk and visit a lot more than we used to. I imagine these letters will mostly be about Hurricane Hazel.

We need to get the letters going again. Even if the telephone lines will be back up soon, I still want to get the letters round to everyone and back to me. Suzy is starting this round with me. We'll send our letters with Marie, who is planning to head back to Raleigh tomorrow. She'll add her letter and bring them to you, Caroline. If you can't post them out from Dix Hill, Marie said she will add yours to hers and take them to Raleigh's main post office. Then they will be coming to you, Annie. I'll bet the Washington post office is up and working. Let's try to get this around as quick as possible.

I mostly want to know how you and your family did in the hurricane. I hate that I can't talk to you to find out if you are all right. That is the number 1 thing I want you to write. Just like I did at the top of this letter. Write first how you are doing.

As you know, Marie's family joined Suzy, me, and Larry in Burlington to wait out the storm. There was a lot of damage, more than we've ever had since living here. We are nearly a week away from it

and have just about cleaned everything
up. We are ready to get the Washerette
open again as soon as the electricity is
back on. We have dirty laundry waiting!

Larry and I have decided to postpone
our move to Surf City until '55. That
seems like a good number. That will
make it 10 years since Larry and I got
married. I guess we can make changes
in our life again. It will be 25 years
since Momma Flo died. Can y'all believe
that? It was 1930. Marie was just a baby.
Caroline, you were only 14. Annie was 17,
and Dianne was 21. I won't say how old I
was 'cause I am younger than I look. What
a life we have had! I've been thinking a
lot about this. Marie's illness, Frank's
terrible car wreck, and this hurricane
made me see how we really don't have
control over our life. We just have to
be ready to swim with the tide.

Back to moving to Surf City. We
bought the property for next to nothing.
And if it is still there, we can make it
livable. Maybe we can even make it bigger
than the place here in Burlington. I
told Larry we will need a guest bedroom
or two so my sisters and their families
can visit every summer. And just so you
see how different I am feeling about
what has happened in our lives, I will
invite Frank, Eli, and maybe Elizabeth
(if she acts right) to visit the beach. I
know it's making your mouth drop to read
that. But I have decided since Frank will
always be Marie's first papa and Eli is
Marie's half-brother, we ought to act
like family.

Larry and me are going to drive to

Surf City after the roads are clear all
the way. Seeing how things are will help
us decide how quickly we should move. If
there is nothing there, we will wait till
the spring to start building back.

Hope to see you at the ree-sort next
summer!

Love you all,
Ethel

From the second half of Burlington, I am
all right!

Hello family,

Oh my God, it was a terrible storm.
Momma made light of it, but I was so
scared! I kept saying since we are all
in these cramped quarters if the house
blows over, there will be nine Nash
people blowing around the neighborhood.
It's a good thing Momma told us to wear
our clothes to bed, or we might have
flown around in our pajamas! Every board
in the house was shaking. The windows
were rattling. I was sure the roof was
coming off.

The next day it was the weirdest
sight. The clearest blue sky you ever
saw. Even in the rubble around our
neighborhood, everything looked clean.
It was like all that rain washed away
any dust and dirt that existed. Did that
happen where you were?

It took most of the day to get
everything put back. We did not flood
or have any roof damage, so we didn't

have to mop up like some neighbors did.
As soon as it looked like they didn't
need me anymore, I went to see my friend
Francie. The yard around her house has
a lot of big old oak trees. Most of them
lost branches. They were scattered all
over the place. Since their house is on a
hill, they didn't flood. I walked through
a fast-running creek near the road that
hadn't been there before. Once I jumped
over the downed tree branches and got to
their front porch, I knocked on the door.
No one answered. After knocking several
times and finding it hard to breathe, I
threw my shoulder into the front door. It
flung open, and I ran through the house.
There was no sound. None.

I shouted their names and asked them
to answer me, but I didn't hear anything
back. Their house is big. Francie's mother
has said many times it was bigger than
they needed. I went running through all
the rooms, then realized I couldn't hear
if they were making quiet noises. I slowed
down and went back through the rooms
again, quietly this time. Nobody was
there, no blood, not even much damage.

Then I remembered there was an
attic. Francie and I would go up there
sometimes. I went up the back stairs
and speaking in a normal tone I said,
"Francie, please be okay. I need you."

The stairs creaked. Even though that
really wasn't unusual, I stopped. I took
a few more steps and listened. I could
hear something that sounded like a moan,
but it might have been the wind or my
imagination. I pushed open the attic door.
It took a minute for my eyes to adjust to

the dim light, then I said, "Hey, it's me, Suzy. Is anybody here? Are you hurt?"

In the little bit of light from the sun coming in through the slats of wood in the A-frame at the peak of the ceiling, I could see a person crouched in the corner with a large wood beam wedged on top of them. I could see Francie's red hair.

Francie and her mother were curled up together in that corner. I shook them both calling their names. They were alive but not awake. I ran down the stairs and out of the house so fast.

I called the neighbors to come. Several people ran toward me. I wasn't sure I was making much sense, but I think I said there were two people hurt in the attic. I was so scared.

One of them said she was a nurse. She shouted for someone named Red to bring her bag to her. Evidently Red was an assistant or husband. He did what he was told. Quick as a rabbit.

Trying to stay out of the way, I sat on the porch step for what seemed like hours. An ambulance arrived. After taking stretchers into the house, they brought out both Francie and Mrs. O'Brien. I ran to Francie and told her to stay alive. She nodded slightly, then in a weak voice said, "I will, Sue."

Family, I'm getting to the point of this horrible story to tell you about the happiness. The nurse came over to me and told me they both would be okay. Apparently, they got knocked out by the beam. She said they just needed to rest overnight at the hospital.

I walked back home and told the story to Momma, Larry, Marie, and Al. To say that there was lots of love spread around is an understatement. They looked as worried as I was.

I announced to them all, "From this time forward, my name is Sue."

I love you all,

Sue

Raleigh Nash Roberts family survived!
Thursday, October 21, 1954

To the Nash, Dixon, Martin, Fox, Walsh, Roberts families,

We should include the Pollard family on the next Round-Robin Letter. Eli Pollard needs to know us. I want my children to know their cousin and their granddad Frank. He is part of the Nash family, even if not by name. As you know, Frank's accident nearly scared the life out of me. Momma and I will visit Frank and Eli as soon as we can get things settled here. And we will be cordial to Elizabeth. Right, Momma?

~~Suzy~~ Sue was right; it was a terrible storm. The news did not predict Hazel would take a more western path than other hurricanes. Being in Burlington was not as safe as we expected, but we were better off being together. Francie is Sue's good friend, an amazing seamstress, and smart woman. When she was hurt, it was as if one of Sue's arms had been ripped off. Her genuine fear was that it could not be reattached.

Al and Papa Larry got to know each other very well. They worked hard to get the house and Kooler businesses up and running. They helped the neighbors cut the trees that had fallen in their yards. Al taught Larry how to play poker. It might not have been a good idea, but there was a lot of solving the world's problems, boasting like a rooster, and deep laugher going on. They played on the picnic table out front. Probably far enough away that we couldn't hear the details of their discussion. As you all know, Momma doesn't like secrets, so she stayed close to the screen door when they were out there. They used pennies as the ante. We will be good as gold if Al can keep winning.

The children seemed to grow up during the last weeks. Jimmy has taken on the role of big brother quite well. Al Jr and Mary are much closer. They often play school together, and Al Jr always lets Mary be the teacher. Mary is quite the disciplinarian around schoolwork. She checks Al Jr's homework every morning. I am not sure what she is having him do, but he is willing. Emma Lou is nearly two months old and so responsive to family. She sleeps most of the night, so I can too. What a difference sleep can make! Now I can concentrate and be nicer.

I began making new plans for us. I talked them over with Al in the car when we returned to Raleigh. The children were all asleep for a bit. I got started by saying, "Al dear, I have somethings to talk over with you. I need to alter the path I am on."

He stared over at me with eyebrows squinched and head lowered and said, "What path? Why change anything?"

"I've had a plan for my life since before I met you. There have been some turns off the path that I did not foresee—falling in love with you, marriage, babies, more babies, and getting sick. And this hurricane. It all came at us, and I haven't taken the time to readjust. You and I just kept moving in the direction we were pulled."

Al was fidgeting in the car seat. His hands held the steering wheel so hard his knuckles were white. He stared at the road in front of him. "What are you talking about, Marie? New clothes? New furniture? Some help?"

I giggled, "Well, now that you mention it, we could use all that, but I know we can't afford it. I'm talking about our future. What do you want for our future?"

His hands relaxed a bit. "Marie, I want to earn enough money that we can buy all the things you want. I have a good job, but now with four children I need to get a second job. Or a better job. I want a bigger house for us. No less than three bedrooms and another bathroom."

He paused for a moment. "Hell yeah, I want to use the bathroom without having to rush it!"

"Me too, Al. I can't remember the last time I took a bath without a child in there with me." We both laughed, easing the stress of the conversation.

I reached over and rubbed Al's neck and said, "I love you, Al. Things won't be like this forever. If it is money we need, I can finish college and get a job with a good salary."

Al thought for about five seconds and said, "Marie, how can you go back to school with the children needing their momma? I can just get another job."

I looked in the back seat. The children were sleeping. Emma Lou was asleep in the front seat between us. I had plenty more time. I pulled out the list from my dress pocket to read to him.

"Here is a draft of the plan I've been thinking about:

1.   Assistant work at NC State College and take classes while the older children are in school.
2.   Once Emma Lou is on the bottle, see if Barbara Lieberman can keep her during the day."

Then I said, "Okay let's talk about those two things first. What do you think?"

Al's muscles got stiff again. His foot was laying heavy on the gas pedal. He didn't have to think too long before he answered. He said, "I think children need their momma. It costs to go back to school. Can a student be an assistant and get paid?"

I responded, hoping I was right. "Yes, I would be paid to assist the professors or work in the offices. I knew some of those students when I was in my freshman year at State College. Remember the money that Frank gave Momma for my college? I think there is enough in that bucket to pay for college to finish my degree.

"Barbara is a great mother and a really good friend. She is kind and loving to children. I trust her. I haven't talked with her about this yet, but we could pay her a little something to keep Emma Lou. Or I could keep her children sometimes on the weekend to pay her back. Besides, it will only be a few hours a day."

A voice from the back seat summoned us. "Momma, Papa, I need a bathroom. Can you pull over?"

Al responded to that pretty quick, ready to change the subject. "That's a good idea. We can all use a walk-about." He pulled the car down the next road and stopped. The backseat of kids unloaded.

Al and I did not get back to that discussion before we reached home. As always, one thing led to another, unpacking, getting the children fed and down for bed, and me doing all of that with Emma Lou wrapped around my body.

After all was settled in, I sat down to write this letter. Caroline agreed to come by tomorrow to see us and take the letters with her. She plans to post them to Annie.

Here is the rest of what was on my plan. But you are the only ones who know. So don't talk to the men about it yet.

3.   Forget the major in engineering. Be practical. Choose one that can get me a job.

4.   Let the older children help with the younger ones. I can't do 4 by myself.

5.   Start saving money toward a new house.

What do y'all think? A good plan? I know Momma will say that "A plan without a way to get it done might as well be a wish."

My last thoughts at the end of this letter are for my dear sister, Sue. Sue, we totally missed celebrating your 24th birthday! We were all under the influence of Hurricane Hazel on October 14th. You really can't fight that. We just did as Hazel commanded, "Get out of the way! I am coming through!"

Listen y'all. This is 1954! Women can now be independent. We can make our own choices. I am so proud of you, my adult sister. You are a successful business woman! I know you are reworking your life plan. My advice to you is to find your true north. It is the direction of magnetic pull on Earth. It is also what can pull you toward home. Home in your heart. Home with your family. Home you want to create. Include in that plan what really matters. Someone who loves you, is truthful and trustworthy, and, most of all, you can't see spending your whole life without. Sometimes we choose someone that others don't accept right away. If it is worth it to you, grab hold of their hand and take them with you through life.

Sue, I left you a birthday gift on your pillow before leaving. It is not extravagant, but it has special meaning from me to you.

Love to all my family!

Marie

From The Hill! I am alive and okay with medication!

Friday, October 22, 1954

To all my relations. Too many to name,

Everybody reading this letter knows about my heroic helpfulness in August! Well, it is two months later, and I had been languishing (new word of the week). Not anymore!! This dang storm made plenty of work for anyone with languishing tendencies (two new words this week).

Raleigh was hit hard too. Dorothea Dix Hospital campus is covered with oak and pecan trees. We love it in the spring when the new leaves start peeking out. We love it in the summer so we can be shaded from the heat. I even love it in the fall because the colors are striking, even though there is leaf raking for all. As you all know, winter is my least favorite season mainly because of the cold. Without the hundreds of trees to build homes in, the squirrel families would freeze to death.

The building administrators (new word for bosses) organized all of us that were able before Hazel arrived. We boarded up windows, moved things that would blow around to the storage buildings, and covered door thresholds (another new word) of the basement doors with sandbags.

I don't remember ever making sandbags before. There is a technique to it. Get military grade fabric, fill half way with sand, not dirt or clay, and don't make them heavier than 35 pounds or you won't be able to move them. Of course, the men at Dix said they could handle 50 pounds, so they made bigger ones. You know what? They were not around the day after the storm when we needed to get the sandbags moved away from the doors. They were assigned to chop down broken trees and cut firewood from branches that were too small to make furniture. It took two of us women to move each bag. We were hauling bags all day. The next day I was so sore I could hardly lift my arms to put on clothes.

Did you know there are over 100 buildings on this campus? I know that because my next assignment was to inspect each for damage that must be fixed. I created a log to prioritize the urgency of the work needed. (How about that kind of organization by the baby Nash sister!) Do you remember Dr. Redmond made me get my driver's license? Now that I can drive legally, I was able to drive from house to house and building to building. I didn't have to walk it.

Last night Joe came over. We hadn't seen each other lately. He has a full-time job with a construction firm in Raleigh and a second job with the works department at Dix. I wasn't home much in August. Then when Marie got better and took baby Emma home, I felt like I didn't have a job anymore. Being without a purpose is new for me. My purpose, as long as I can remember, was to get better. To be an adult. See doctors, go to therapy, take my medicine, cook and clean up for myself. After spending that time with my sisters being helpful, I realized I don't have to rely on others so much. That I should grow myself. Guess what? I started taking some college classes!!! How about that?

You know they have school here. Just like every kid in North Carolina, if we are fit, we have to get an education. Marie and Suzy, you may not know this, but I have been here since I was 15 years old. I took all my high school requirements here with all the other nutty people.

They have teachers from NC State College come teach some college classes at night. I started in September taking English and Math classes. Since the teachers are real professors, I get college credit for the classes. Hey Marie, when you come back to college, maybe we can hang out in the campus lunchroom.

You may have noticed I am using new words—college words. My English professor said I need to work on broadening my vocabulary. Each week I have to choose and use five unfamiliar complex words at least ten times. I can choose which words to use, but she has to approve them. Evidently four-letter words are no longer cool.

Ethel knew I enrolled as a college student back in August. The first thing she asked was, "How are you going to pay for this?" I reminded her of the money I had gotten from our momma's estate and wages I have gotten for jobs I've had. I have nowhere to spend money, so it has been piling up in the bank. This seems like a good way to use it.

Anyway, back to Joe. I cooked a bounty of vegetables, which needed to be harvested after the storm. He brought some fish, all scaled and cleaned. He caught them in the river next to the railroad track. We talked until late in the evening about Hazel, work, my classes, and how life is changing for us both. Joe will be my life-long best friend. He is a good man and knows a lot about the world, construction, and fixing all things mechanical. Joe the handyman. That's what he is.

Ethel, tell Larry that Joe is happy to help build The Kooler when he can get away from work. He said construction work gets slow in winter, so he can take some time to go to Topsail Island. Just call and let us know the condition of the house when you arrive there.

Sue, I am sorry your friend Francie got hurt. It is scary when people close to you get hurt and you don't know how to help. I felt that when Marie and Frank were in the hospital. All this mess reminded me that modern medicine is amazing. I am a living specimen (notice that word) of that. Without the advances in mental health, I am sure I would not have become the person I am. Plus without my sisters' loyalty, I might be irrelevant. (How do you like that for a deep word?)

I can't wait to hear your voices over the phone. Soon. Very soon.

Love,
Your relevant Caroline

The Washington crew is battered and bruised, but we are building back!

Monday November 1, 1954

My dearest Ethel, Caroline, Marie, Suzy, and all others,

What a time we have all had! None of us came out of the past two months unscathed. (Caroline, there's a word for you!)

I am just happy to know all of you are okay, considering . . .

This letter reached me after the telephones were back up, but I held off calling y'all so I could at least record my part of this round of letters.

Ethel cheated though. She called me last night. She said electric and phones were back up in her neighborhood. Mainly, she wanted me to know they are leaving for Surf City today. She said November 1st sounded like a good day to move on.

Sue, we talked about you a bit. She is worried about you. But is trying to work through this new thing she called "man/woman confusion." I'll call you later this week, and we can talk more. Just know we all love you very much, whatever comes of this.

The children, Jon, and I went to the Pentagon before the storm. It's one of the strongest buildings in the U.S. We were fine. It was quite an adventure camping in Jon's office. With Hazel being such a fast mover, we really didn't have to stay hunkered down very long. They called all clear midday on Saturday, October 16. Actually, it was not "clear" outside. The courtyard in the center of the Pentagon looked like a bomb had dropped. The military was called right away to take care of the streets in and around the city.

Hazel was a menace in DC. High winds tore up trees all over the Capitol and White House grounds. The Potomac River rose over its banks, adding to the flooding from rain. You may have seen those pictures in the news. It was pretty dramatic.

After the parking lot and roads were clear enough, we went home to Arlington. Our neighborhood had destruction everywhere. Most of the houses outside the city are newer and not built as solid as the DC neighborhoods. As we approached our neighborhood, roof shingles were all over the place, windows were broken, and siding from one house landed in the yard of another. Jon skirted around all the debris on the streets. He turned the corner and drove up the hill to our house. It was awful. On the front, part of the porch was missing, windows were blown out, and much of the roof was torn off. I was worried about what the inside was going to look like. I found it hard to breathe. My chest hurt.

Up until this time, there was little noise from the children. We were all in shock. Then Lisa began crying. She shouted, "Papa, my swing is gone!"

"Where is the front door? Look at the windows!" Jon Jr shouted.

Eight-year-old Dianne just whimpered and stared.

Jon put his hand on my shoulder and said, "We are going to be okay, children. Right, Momma?"

I took my hands from my face and turned around so I could see the children's faces. "We aren't the only ones struck by Hurricane Hazel. We are safe. All can be fixed."

Then Dianne reminded us of what really mattered. "Momma, do you think Lelia is alive? Did Hazel tear up her house while she was in it?"

Jon stopped the car and turned off the ignition. He bowed his head and said, "Let's pray for all who were in this storm."

We started the Lord's Prayer as sincere as if we were sitting in church.

I wanted to know if all my family made it. I wanted to know if Hazel went to West Virginia where Lelia was. I wanted to know how we were going to recover from this tragedy.

Jon turned to the backseat pointing his finger at the children and said, "Stay in the car. Momma and I will go look around inside. I will tell you when it is safe to come in. Do not open the car door. Do you hear me?"

In unison, all three children said, "Yes, Papa."

Jon came around and opened the car door on my side. As I stepped out of the car, I grabbed his hand for stability. We walked slowly. Jon kicked things out of the way. Examining the damage done to our home made me shiver. When we got inside, it was obvious rain had come through the windows and roof. The furniture was soaked and pushed out of place. The kitchen was the worst. Cabinets had fallen away from the walls. All the glass in the windows was on the floor. It did not look like a kitchen. It was a pile of rubble. My eyes came to rest on Lisa's swing seat. It had come through the glass windows and landed on the dining room table. It crashed among dinner dishes from the last night we ate there.

Without even checking on the sturdiness of the stairs, Jon rushed up to the children's rooms. I went outside to check on the children. Jon Jr started to open the back seat car door. I shook my head, "No! It's not safe!"

I grabbed the door handle and slid in the back seat. Reaching as far around them as I could, I pulled them into my arms. "The house is really damaged. It will take a long time to find all our things. We need your help. You must be strong. Keep praying for others, not for our things. Things don't matter."

Before I seal this letter, let me tell you something marvelous.

As the sun began to set on the 15th day after

Hazel came, the children were sitting at the
kitchen table we had managed to repair. They were
drawing, writing, or just playing with pieces
of toys. I was proud of them figuring out how to
occupy their time with very little.

My body and mind were exhausted. I needed
to be alone to think. "Children, I will be right
back. I just need to sit awhile."

I left the kitchen. Staggering out to the
side porch, I lowered my weary body to the
top step. With my elbows on my knees, I put my
forehead in my hands. Trying to rebuild strength,
I began quietly talking to all of you and to Momma
and Dianne in heaven.

Then I heard a car approaching. I was
squinting against the sunset. I wondered who must
be coming back to reconstruct their lives as we
were trying to do. It was an older truck. I could
make out that there were people in the truck
bed and three people in the front seat. I could
not see their faces. The truck rumbled into our
driveway. I raised my hand to shield my eyes from
the sun and called out, "Hello. Can I help you?"

A woman jumped from the back of the truck and
started running toward the house. "No, ma'am, we
are hoping we can help you." It was Lelia's voice.

I ran to her and grabbed her small body.
"Thank you, dear God!"

As we both cried in each other's arms, she
replied, "Thank you, Jesus! We are alive!"

Ethel, Caroline, and all others in our family,
I know we will be changed forever by this. We
can't be together right now. Please let's plan on
Christmas together. Somewhere. Somehow.

Merry Christmas real soon!

Annie

CHAPTER 15 — NOVEMBER 1954

Ethel
Surf City, Here We Come

IT HAS BEEN THREE WEEKS since Hurricane Hazel destroyed much of North Carolina. Me and Larry decided to drive southeast to see how bad it was at our coastal property. It's 200 miles or so as the crow flies. Of course, we ain't flying, so Larry figured it would take us about four hours if the roads were clear. I packed for eating twice on the road. Larry decided to keep close to the towns where we might be able to get gas on the way. Which will also cut down on the number of times we have to use the roadside for emergencies.

I was the map reader since Larry liked to drive. I had to have something to occupy me because he scared the livin' daylights outta me when he was the driver. Whenever I suck in my breath or make a movement with my hands to warn him of something, he reminds me he is an experienced long-haul trucker.

"I know how to drive, Ethel. Calm yourself, woman!" he says.

That would usually make me grab a magazine to read or pick up the map and shake it. I told him I couldn't help it. I was just too dang nervous!

As we drove through southeastern North Carolina, we saw houses turned upside down. Fields of cotton that had not been harvested looked like swamp crops. We passed by a town called Turkey. I am sure there were none of those left. The long poultry buildings were blown around like sticks. No turkeys to be seen. Outside a town named Kenansville, old planation homes were covered in downed trees. The older the place, the less that was left.

I asked Larry where he thought all the people were. The roads were empty except for a tractor or farm truck here and there. I was surprised not seeing anybody working to fix things.

He was thinking the same way. He thought it was weird too. He said maybe they took cover in other cities or with family that live somewhere else like we did when we headed west out of harm's way. We didn't go quite far enough, but we fared better than these people.

Thinking out loud, I told Larry that if Al Jr had been with us, he'd have been wondering about the animals. It is all so terrible. I don't know how long we should wait to bring the grandkids here. Larry said maybe next summer.

My insides were tied up in knots. I felt dizzy and sick at my stomach. I didn't even want any of the coffee I had brought along.

"Larry, I feel sick. We might need to stop at the

next filling station. One with a bathroom. I don't think I want to eat, but I'll get it out for you."

Luckily, it only took a few miles to find a filling station. We got a fill-up and used the facilities. Larry ate ham biscuits and tomato and cucumber salad. I just drank a glass of milk to calm my stomach.

We got back on the road, but the view did not change. Route 210 was winding all around. The road seemed to be following the rivers.

"Larry, I don't think I've ever passed over so many rivers and creeks in one trip. President Roosevelt's New Deal should've had road building in this area on their project list."

"That's probably why the water is still hanging around. The soil is holding the water, and this is a low part of the state. These people have to make a living farming on this land. I don't know how they do it."

I thought back to our farm in Wilson County. We rarely saw floods. Reminding us both I said, "We are so fortunate, Larry. I've never seen land like this. How will they survive here?"

Larry's voice got quiet, almost like he was praying. "I don't know, Ethel. It'll be different for us."

I hoped he was right. I made a promise to myself to never be poor. Maybe our family was poor when I was young, but us kids didn't know it. We didn't have a lot, but we had what we needed.

I figured it would take months for these people to build back. From this moment on I vow to always keep at least six month's living money tucked away.

It was getting dark. If I was following the map right,

we were nearly there. Up ahead was Holly Ridge. Camp Davis, the old army base, was there. Caroline's Joe told us he was stationed there until '48. He's been back to Topsail Island a few times since and encouraged us to buy property there. He was the one who told Larry he was sure Surf City will be a booming seaside resort soon. He convinced Larry get in on it while the prices are low.

"Larry, do you remember that Joe Kirkpatrick said we should get into this resort?"

He smiled a bit and said, "Yeah. That's why we're heading this way. We'll get in on it while the gettin's good! Come hell or highwater, Ethel, together we will make something of this!"

I was feeling better once we crossed the bridge to the island. I could see lights ahead and people crossing the streets. There was a store where people were buying food and materials. I even saw a few cars driven by what looked like teenagers out for the fun of it. We were entering a town that was already bouncing back from what Hazel had done to them.

Reassuring us both, I announced, "Holy moly, Larry. Look at this place. These people are coming back from the nightmare."

He leaned over and kissed my cheek. "Yes ma'am. And we will too. Are you ready?"

"I'm ready, Larry. We can be these people. We are these people!"

———

After a good night's sleep in the small motel room that Larry arranged, I felt happiness cover me like a quilt. I breathed deeply, filling my lungs with moist, warm air. It smelled like salty country ham on a dinner table. I just lay there for a while, thinking about this adventure. Was it going to be awful or awesome?

The sun began to peek through the curtains. I turned toward Larry and rubbed his belly. "Let's get some coffee and breakfast at the shop next door. Then I want to see our bungalow in paradise."

He said, "Why not do a little lovin' before we go? We should get our money's worth outta this motel."

"Why not . . . ." I replied.

When we left the hotel room, I was starving. I couldn't wait any longer. While Larry was packing our stuff back in the boot of the car, I grabbed the last few baloney sandwiches and apples from the cooler. I poured sweet tea from the thermos, and we sat at a picnic table outside the motel. It was a celebration meal.

Raising the cup to my good man and using my dreamy eyes look, I whispered, "I love you, Larry Martin. Here's to our new life."

Larry just quietly gave me a big kiss.

It only took a few minutes to get to where we were going. I had not seen the house yet, but I expected I would know it when I saw it. Larry was so darn excited about the place that he had described it a hundred times.

He pulled the car into a yard. "Ethel, there it is. It's small, but it's ours!"

I replied, "And it is still standing. It's a short little thing. Maybe that's why it made it. It hugs the ground."

There was a lot of sand blown up against its foundation. Glass was blown out of the plate-glass windows. No doubt there would be water inside. I grabbed Larry's hand, and we stood there and admired our beat-up little home.

We turned around taking it all in. Sand covered everything. The old army warehouse next door to our place had some damage to its roof and siding. But it was there. Hurricane Hazel hadn't taken it down. A good sign. Other houses were not as lucky. Down the road in both directions were buildings that looked like they blew or floated away from their original foundation. One house across the road fared as well as our place. A woman was sweeping sand to the road from her porch and sidewalk. Seemed like a bigger job than one broom could handle. I guess sometimes you just need to do something. No matter how small the step. I waved to her. She waved back.

Looking past the woman sweeping, I realized there must be an ocean over there. "Larry, let's go see the ocean. It's a warm November day. I want to put my feet in that water."

We headed toward the noise of waves crashing on the beach. I picked up my pace until I was almost running. Larry was behind me. We climbed the dunes and stood at the top.

Larry was looking over at the town. I turned him around and said, "Let's look at this first. Soak in the wonder of it all. We can look at the battered and bruised island next."

As we got higher on the dune, I could see the gorgeous blue water. The sun had fully risen over the horizon. My eyes filled with warm tears. I gasped at the sight of it. "Larry, look at that. Just look at that sunrise. How can anything be impossible when you can see that every day?"

He put his arms around me and squeezed. "I can't wait for the kids to see this. They won't believe it either."

We walked arm in arm down the dune, toward the sea. I was so overcome by the beauty of the ocean I had not noticed the catastrophe that Hazel caused on the beach. Larry held tight to me as we stepped over debris that had washed up from the ocean. When I reached the water, I took off my shoes and let the water drown my feet. It was soft and warm. Weirdly warm.

After a few minutes of standing there comforted by the sun and the water, I decided I could now turn and look at reality.

Larry walked toward a structure that looked like it used to be a fishing pier. It was torn to shreds. Turning his back to the ocean, he studied the buildings built high on the dunes. Few were left whole. The wreckage thrown all over the beach reminded me that lives were ruined by Hazel. Nearly every inch of white sand was covered by pieces of houses, wood pilings from the pier, mountains of underwater grass, dead sea animals, and shells by the hundreds. Looking north, we could see buildings that had fallen facedown onto the beach when the dunes they were built on were erased underneath them.

In the distance, we could hear machines cranking and moving. We climbed the dunes toward the noise. Tractors were coming through pushing sand and rubble from the roads and parking areas back toward the beach. The workers were giving the sand back to the ocean. Back where it belonged.

As I started down the steep dune toward the road, I decided sliding might be the best way. I sat on my bottom, pushed my body forward with my hands, yelling, "Wheee!! Here I go!"

At the end of the sandhill there was a small crowd watching me. People were looking at me like I was crazy. To prove them right, I stood with both arms high in the air and yelled, "Goodbye, Hazel! Hello tomorrow!"

From the top of the dune, Larry started clapping and shouting, "Yes, sirree! Hazel is gone. Good riddance! Surf City is back!"

Everyone on the streets started shouting and clapping. Among the crowd, I noticed a man in a police-type uniform raise a bent arm and yell above the others. "Oorah!"

There was more hollering of that word back and forth to one another. It seemed like a strange language, but most people in Surf City knew it.

Larry and I found our way back to our place. I opened the boot of the car and grabbed us both a Pepsi. We downed them like it was the first drink we'd had in decades. I stared at Larry, then stared at the house. I was trying to imagine us living there, the grandchildren playing in the yard, and me serving ice cream out the front window. It was a hard picture to paint given what it looked like now.

I made my way to the side door and pushed back the screen door. It fell off its hinges smashing to the ground. We both laughed. I put the key in the door lock and turned it until I heard the click. A little worried it would also fall off its hinges, I pushed gently at first. It did not budge.

Through my laughter I said, "Larry, she is short, she is sturdy, she is also stubborn."

Then with all my might I shoved my body into the door. It flung open but held sturdy to the frame.

Larry let out a chuckle. "She's a lot like you, missy!"

I stood as tall as I could, looked back at Larry, and stared into his eyes. Without words I was letting him know we had one more chance to change our minds.

He put his hand on my head, nodded once and said, "Are you ready, Mrs. Martin?"

I grinned. "I'm ready, Mr. Martin."

He bent down, put one arm around my back and the other behind my knees. Lifting me like I didn't weigh much, he walked us both into the house.

I leaned my head on this chest and said, "Oh, my gentle giant. Thanks for convincing me to do this. At least for now."

All afternoon we cleared and cleaned like we did in Burlington two weeks ago. Remembering Caroline's job at Dix Hill after the storm, I pulled some paper and a pencil out of my pocketbook. I began taking inventory of every room.

- Front room—replace sheet glass, repair ceiling where it leaked, replace floor tile
- Kitchen—fix or replace stove, rebuild cabinets, buy table and chairs, get a telephone installed, replace window glass, replace floor. Is it rotten?
- Bathroom— just clean, floor looks okay
- Hallway to back of house—replace floor, can see the sand below the house through the holes in the boards
- Bedroom 1—replace floor like the hall, new furniture. Will two double beds fit in there? repair closet door
- Bedroom 2—same as bedroom 1 but larger—buy a double bed and a set of twin bunks for when the family visits
- Back room/living room—replace or repair floor, buy and install new sheet glass for windows, paneling on the walls, new door, add a screen door

Larry and I met at the side door. I held out my list, and he showed me his. He had done the same on the outside. We are two peas in a pod.

Larry wanted to get down to the bottom line. "Let me work on these tonight to see how much money it's all gonna cost. Then we need to decide what's the most important."

For our second night in Surf City, there was no motel room. We slept on the newly cleaned bedroom floor. A pallet of blankets, sheets and pillows was our motel bed.

The sunrise zoomed into the house through broken wood siding and naked windows. I stood to study its color. It was like tangerines and lemons on a clear blue cloth.

"Good beautiful morning to you, paradise!" I said.

Larry and the car were gone. By the looks of it, he had not come to bed at all. The kitchen floor was littered with pieces of paper. He evidently calculated all night. I could not find a final page with numbers. He must have taken it with him. On the bathroom door was a note from him.

Ethel,

I've gone to look for materials and prices. I will head to Camp Lejeune to see if I can get wood and nails to board up the place. I'll be back late.

You're my best girl,
Larry

Best girl? Who are the other girls?

Since I had the day to myself, I decided I may as well walk around the town and meet people. It looks like we're gonna put down roots. We better see who these folks are.

I met the mayor, a realty & construction business owner, and a "Topsul" Island historian. They were all the same person. Mr. A. H. Ward. BINGO! A great person to know. He gave me a lot of information about the island, and I told him about us. He knew Wilson County and had been to Raleigh a few times, but never to Burlington.

I told him about our place and the list of repairs needed. I said, "Larry's headed to Camp Lejeune scrouging for supplies. Our plan is to someday open an ice cream business and a washerette."

Mr. Ward smiled at the plan. "That's a heck of a combination. We need both of those here. When your husband comes back, y'all come see me. I think I can help."

I was floating on cloud nine! I had met the man of our dreams!

My stomach was growling, so I stopped in a restaurant that was set on the dunes. The road that brought us onto the island ended right beside this place. What a good location! Looked like they were up and running. Much of the building was boarded up, but I found a table to sit at where I could watch the ocean. It was way past lunchtime, and I was tired of sandwiches. I ordered fried fish and fried potatoes. And just for the heck of it, I asked for a Budweiser even though there were lots of beers to choose from. Goooodness! Like Larry said, this was a ree-sort!

The rest of the afternoon I walked around saying hey to people. I met folks named Medlin, Batts, Yow, Paliotti, Stubbs, and more names than I could remember. I was surprised to see folks with names that clearly said they were from all kinds of places. I asked just about all of them how they found this place. Mostly it was from being stationed here during the war. Not a one gave me the brush-off. We all had a lot to talk about, starting with how bad Hurricane Hazel had hit North Carolina.

I decided to walk back to the house. Maybe Larry would be back. Sure enough, our car was parked in the yard. Right next to it was an older model red truck full of wood slats, boards, a table, and some chairs. He must have landed a valuable friend!

I hollered, "Well, lookie here! Is that for us?"

A skinny black man stood up from the other side of the truck. He waved a hand, nodded his head, and said, "Yes ma'am, it is. I had this stuff left over. Mr. Martin said you could use it."

As I got closer to the truck, I could see household items in there. Drawers full of kitchen utensils, dishes, pots and pans. I pulled out a pretty pink ceramic lamp. "Well, I'll be darn. Thank you, young man. Larry paid you for this, didn't he?"

"Yes ma'am. He paid a fair price and filled up the truck twice. I'm gonna help him move this load inside and head back home."

Larry stepped out of the side door of the house and introduced me, "Ethel, this is Sam. He lives in Holly Ridge. He was out by his house selling stuff, so I stopped. Sam, I see you met my wife, Ethel. I bought all he had, but needed him to haul it for me. This is our third trip. Wait till you see what we got!"

I was concerned. "Sam, why were you selling all this stuff?"

Larry gave me that "hush now" look.

Sam said, "We lost most of our house in the storm. Whatever we could collect that blew all over the place, we piled up to sell. Me, my wife, and kids are moving to her momma's house in the Appalachian Mountains. We can't carry it and don't need it."

Larry stood tall in the doorframe of the house.

"Ethel, can you believe our luck? I drove by and saw Sam and his family pulling this stuff to the front of their yard. Even young ones were out there working. I pulled in the yard and asked if I could help. He told me his story, and I told him mine. We decided we could help each other out."

That tall skinny man looked like a tired angel to me. I walked to him and gave him a hug. Clearly it was not what he expected. "Well, Sam, this is just what we needed. I am sorry you lost your house. You are one of God's angels."

Sam took a step back from me, bowed his head slightly, and said, "Your husband is the messenger from God. He came just at the right time. My wife just about gave up. Now we can head out with money in our pocket. Praise the Lord."

I looked back at Larry with his large frame and big belly standing tall. At that moment he was the most handsome thing in the world. A good man is a handsome man.

Marie
Preparing to Gather

WE NEEDED A NASH FAMILY Christmas. We needed to gather together.

Christmas is on Saturday this year. That worked perfectly. My momma, her sisters, and I talked endlessly on the phone once this was decided. Since Caroline and I live in Raleigh, we agreed to take the lead.

A few nights in early December, I dialed up each family unit announcing the plans. I told all the women to bring their men to the telephone so they could hear me too. I typed up what I was going to say because I wanted the same instructions heard each time. That is just what Momma would do just like she did when the Nash Round-Robin Letters began. Rules make expectations clear.

Hello family! Every adult should be on this call. It is up to the parents to keep the children involved in the arrangements of our Grand Nash Christmas. Please bring all people over 20 years old close to the telephone. Can everyone hear me? Answer me with your name so I know you are there. (pause)

You probably already know we have moved heaven and earth to get everyone together the weekend of Christmas 1954 in Raleigh. Ethel, Annie, and Caroline as the eldest agreed it can happen and will happen.

Ethel's words are, "There can be no excuses about needing to go to work or not having time. Everyone should be here—for the whole weekend! No grumbling from anyone!"

This has been a tough year for all of us, some more than others. I get to claim pitiful here. But not the most pitiful. After all, I got a sweet baby out of my tragedy. Daddy Frank earns the first most pitiful award. He almost died.

We all survived Hurricane Hazel and are rebuilding in many different ways. Caroline said to me, "I want this to be a time to spread glue all around (metaphorically of course). We need to bond across the cousin line, aunt and uncle line, and the I-intend-to-or-am-married into the Nash family line." (pause for laughter)

The Walsh family agreed to bankroll the hotel/motel rooms for Ethel & Larry, Suzy & Francie (don't pause for surprise breaths), Annie & Jon and their children. Also, I asked them to get one more room, just in case. Thank you, Jon and the United States Government!

Caroline has arranged a wonderful house for us on the Dix Hill campus. Women will gather at the house by noon on the 24th of December to begin decorating and cooking. Men and children are to arrive by four with Christmas tree in hand. Caroline will show you where on the property you can cut one down.

Everyone, bring a few of your favorite tree ornaments for this Grand Nash tree. Momma said she has Grandma Flo's Christmas angel they used and it will be placed at the top once again. I am bringing lights. The children will finish the tree with the tinsel.

The present you give others should be wrapped in your most creative style. For the children, let's not, as Momma says, "go hog wild." I want the children to remember this Christmas as a most wonderful time together, not for how many or how expensive their gifts were. Don't forget Santa will bring things during the night.

Christmas morning no one will "open" Santa gifts until we all arrive. So, us old folks have to get up early. Everyone, get back to the house by eight thirty a.m. Annie, Caroline, me, and Momma will cook breakfast. Larry, Jon, Joe, and Al are responsible for Christmas lunch. (pause for appropriate grunting and moaning)

That's it for now! Any questions can be answered by the elder sisters because they have been in on this for weeks. I love you all. We are going to make it the best Christmas ever!!

I finished the last call the evening of the fifteenth of December. I was pleased with how all the calls went. Everyone seemed happy to cooperate. There was no moaning at all, or they did it silently. I went to the kitchen and opened the bottle of champagne I had been saving for a special event. Having the Nash family branches by generation and marriage in one place is certainly worth celebrating. Momma said that hadn't happened since everyone moved away from the home place and that was not long after I was born.

I'm not sure if it was the champagne or just exhilaration, but my imagination took me back to a time I was too young to remember. I envisioned the house where Momma and her sisters grew up. I remembered the stories Momma told about her and Frank falling in love. From descriptions Aunt Annie told me, I was picturing Frank, in anticipation of me being born, painting Momma's bedroom two colors so one side would be mine and the other hers. In a trunk somewhere, I have the curtain Momma hung between the two parts of the room for privacy. Not sure who needed the privacy. Frank never stayed there with us.

Frank has explained the reasons he left Momma and me and went to school in Virginia many times. His parents gave him an ultimatum. It was an impossible situation. They told him, "Marry that girl and we disown you! You have no money and no way to finish school. You are a disgrace to our family. You must leave town. No one can know you knocked up a girl like her."

Those words are seared in my memory. I am sure they are for Momma too. Horrible things to say.

Frank told Momma he could make this work. He'd have his parents pay his way to finish school. Then he would bring us to live in Virginia with him.

Momma always told me Frank had dreams. Those dreams made him think he could work it all out. But she said the Pollards were more powerful than love. They locked Frank into their plan. School was paid only month by month. There were people on the inside that reported to Frank's parents how well Frank was following through with their plan. They withheld money from the school and Frank when he began waiver from the agreement. The dream began to crumble.

According to Aunt Annie, and I believe it to be true, Momma turned her back on Frank. Aunt Annie said, "She refused to be a pawn in the Pollard game. She felt not only neglected by the Pollards but also by Frank. She stopped talking to Frank. Although your momma did not move away from the homeplace until we sold it, she moved away from the possibility of ever being a family with Frank."

Thinking about it all made me more determined to help unite our families now. Momma and I had talked about visiting Frank after his recovery from the wreck, but she made all kind of excuses not to go.

I searched for the telephone book where I had written numbers I do not know by heart. I had one more call to make tonight.

———

Caroline and I talked every day about the Christmas plans. Caroline was now the organized Nash sister, and she took it seriously. A new list was made every day. We would divide up the duties based on who could make it happen that day. She would check off the list on the following morning call and start a new list for the day.

As soon as he heard from Momma what we were planning, Larry sent me money. The note in the envelope with the check was so Larry.

Baby girl, this is going to cost an arm and a leg. I don't want you or Caroline to lose any body parts over a party. I love you for doing this for the family.

Larry – dad

P.S. Don't tell your momma how much this is.

We were approaching Christmas Eve. One more day. I was anxious about leaving out some important detail or another. Al and the kids knew it. They stayed away while I was at the kitchen table making lists, checking them off, and moving fast all over the house. I was impatient with them all.

Al Jr let me know they understood. Nearly tiptoeing into the kitchen where I was working, he said "Momma, can I fix lunch for me and the kids? Jimmy said he was starving. But you don't need to do it. I know how to make sandwiches."

My body stiffened. Not in anger, but guilt. I took in my surroundings. I could hear no sounds from the children. Not even a baby crying. "Oh crap." I said to myself. "What kind of mother am I?"

I asked, "Where is your daddy?"

"He's out getting things for the party."

"Where is Emma Lou?" I was ashamed I didn't know the answer to that question.

"Daddy took her over to Mrs. Lieberman's house with the baby bag and bottles. She's fine, Momma." My dear seven year old knew what was going on better than the momma.

Tears began to well up in my eyes. I stood up, pressing my skirt with my hands and breathing deeply. I decided I better act like a responsible person.

"Yes, Al, let's fix some lunch for all of us. You get the bread, and I will find the mayonnaise, baloney, and cheese for you and Mary. I will make Jimmy a plate of his usual—apple slices, grapes, and macaroni." I think I was trying to show I knew about my children.

Al grabbed the peanut butter and raisins. He went to the refrigerator for celery sticks. "Momma, I want to make ants on a log. That always makes Mary laugh."

Mary came into the kitchen, pulling her little brother's hand. "Ants on a log! Gross!" She and Jimmy burst out laughing. Jimmy loves his big sister so much that he laughs whenever she does.

In a sing-song voice, little Al added to the fun. "Ants on a log! Ants for us to eat! Mary loves ants on a log!"

We all were laughing and dancing around the very small kitchen. Singing and laughing. Nothing like laughter, deep belly hilarity, to break the spell of stressing about things.

The rest of the day I was determined to focused on my abandoned children. I assigned Mary and Al separate places in the house to finish up the Christmas presents they were making for each other. Jimmy was in his high chair sampling the cookies I made early in the week. Realizing I didn't even include the children in that cookie making, I thought to myself, "Bad Momma."

I went to the radio to find some Christmas music. As I was turning the dial, I paused on the news. They were saying, "Doctors in Boston performed a kidney transplant . . . ."

"Well, I'll be darn. A transplant," I said and kept turning the dial. I needed to know more about that, but the children didn't.

The dial hit what I was looking for. Perry Como

was singing "There's No Place Like Home for the Holidays." I turned the volume way up and hummed along. Then I had a thought.

I picked up the telephone and dialed Caroline's number.

In a whimsical voice she answered on the first ring. "Hello, this is Caroline Nash, party planner. To whom am I speaking?"

I giggled. "Auntie, it's me. Marie. I just had a great idea for the Christmas house."

It was not funny to her. "Jeez, Marie! I can't add another thing to this list. It's too much stress already! I had to take an extra pill this morning to keep me from screaming at Joe."

I snickered. "Whew, boy, I know what you mean. But this idea will make it all feel better. Is there a radio at the Christmas house we will be using? I think we will need Christmas music playing all weekend."

Caroline paused a moment. "Dang. I haven't played Christmas music in days. Mainly because I have been running around. But also I just forgot it was Christmas in the middle of all this work. I'll ask Joe to handle that for us. As a party planner, I am learning how to delegate."

"Yeah, I've noticed you're mastering that skill. Okay, great. Gotta go. Bye."

Caroline ended the call by restoring my sanity. "Marie, you are the best in the world to help me with this. You are a momma, wife, and all-around smart lady. Thank you for working so hard to juggle it all. See you tomorrow around ten-ish. Once Ethel and

Annie arrive, we will have lots of help with the details. I am so excited about this. It is going to be GRAND!"

Annie
A Grand Nash Christmas Eve

WE CHOSE THE HOTEL NASH for our overnights. It is not fancy, but the name is Nash. What could be more fitting for this gathering even though they're no relation to us? And it's downtown, which places it near Dix Hill. After our families arrived, Ethel and I left the men at the hotel. Ethel warned them not to drink before they finished their chores and arrived with the Christmas tree. My children were with us because Ethel said the children need to be with womenfolk.

I argued, "Oh good golly, sister, this is the twentieth century! Womenfolk? Sheeze! The men have responsibilities too."

"I'm right, aren't I? The menfolk can't do but one thing at a time. And looking after children adds three more things."

I tried to settle things. "Okay, we take Lisa, little Jon, and Dianne with us. We have tons of things to do. They'll be running around unsupervised at The Hill. Is that better?"

"Heck yeah!" Ethel responded.

I can't win. We arrived at the address Caroline had given us looking like gypsies with a carload of children, Nash sisters, boxes of decorations, food, presents, and lots more.

I relaxed when I saw Marie's children sitting on the porch looking very bored in their heavy coats, mittens, and winter caps. When they realized we were their gypsies, Al Jr, with Jimmy in tow, jumped up and came running toward the car.

Mary screamed as she went running into the house. "The Nashes are here! Momma, they came!"

Ethel squirmed out of the car and took off running to the children. Her arms outstretched saying, "Hell yeah, we are here! We said we'd come, didn't we!"

As she was grabbing little Al and Jimmy into her arms, I realized it had been too long since we had seen them.

Stepping out of the driver's seat, I yelled at Ethel, "Stop cussing in front of the children, Ethel!" I pulled open the back door of the car and out came my gaggle of geese running toward the house.

Without thinking, I lowered myself to my sister's foul mouth and shrieked, "Damn. Look at how beautiful you all are! And you're ours!"

I bent down to grab as many children as I could in my hug.

The screen door on the house slammed. Out came more Nashes. Marie was cradling Emma Lou. Suzy was holding a tray of drinks, and another woman was holding her arm. That must be Francie. Caroline, wearing an apron, rushed to us with a dishtowel in one hand, looking like our momma. She opened her arms wide to bring us in.

My children ran inside the house, hugging their cousins and giggling and jumping up and down.

They all were beautiful. This was the picture of family.

All of a sudden Christmas had new meaning to me. It is not just Walshes. Christmas is everyone that loves a Nash.

My children begged the Roberts children to come outside to play. Caroline was in agreement. "Wrap up warm, and I'll show you where you can play."

Caroline gave the orders about safety. "You older ones are in charge of the younger ones. I put bats, baseballs, jump ropes, and a kickball out there. Y'all play together nice. Jimmy and Emma Lou will stay with us. Now go and act like cousins!"

After we got all the stuff unloaded and into the house, Caroline gave us a tour of the place. It was perfect. Spacious and furnished with antiques and worn furniture. It felt like home.

We gathered in the kitchen to enjoy the drinks that Suzy prepared. It turned out to be champagne. I looked at Ethel and smirked.

She knew what I meant. "Okay, Annie. I didn't mean that we couldn't have a drink. It was just the men I was talking about. Moderation is not a word in their vocabulary."

Francie raised her hand that held the glass to begin a toast. We all raised a glass.

She cleared her throat as if uneasy. "I just want to thank you. You are kind to allow me to join the Nash Christmas. I hardly know how to say it but . . ."

Suzy, I mean Sue, stepped beside her and touched her glass to Francie's. Francie continued, "I mean, this is the most amazing family I have ever seen. And you let me be here. To be included. It is so nice."

I tried to help her feel less nervous. "Francie, I've never met you, but I love you. It is just perfect that you join us. The Grand Nash Christmas of 1954 in this fantastic house at The Hill should include anyone that loves a Nash."

Everyone tipped a glass and acknowledged I was right. "Hear, hear!"

After the toast, Caroline handed her full glass to Ethel. She never drinks alcohol. A few years ago, she told Ethel and me that the handfuls of medicine she takes every day make her loopy already. "Liquor would not be a good idea. It would be like I was on the spinning ride at the State Fair. All gaga and throwing up everywhere," she said.

I hoped she had not learned that the hard way.

Evidently Marie thought we needed to change course. She asked Caroline to show off her leadership skills. "Caroline, how about you tour everyone around the place and tell them what we still need to do? I'll bring in the children for lunch."

Like privates led by a sergeant in the army, we all fell in line following Caroline.

I hesitated and turned to Marie. "May I take Emma Lou? I want to hold that beautiful girl."

Marie went to the door and let out a familiar whistle. I stopped mid-step. Growing up, Momma and Daddy always had a certain whistle to bring us into the house. It sounded like a loud whippoorwill call. I still used it with my children but didn't know any of my sisters did. Clearly, they did. I looked out the front window. After the second whistle, I watched each child raise their head and look toward the mother-call. Marie did not speak. She moved her arms above her head to summon them inside. They came running. Wow, that was cool!

Ethel prepared lunch for Jimmy and Emma Lou. Marie brought out all the essentials and laid them on the counter. She told the other children to fix their own. I was not sure my children could do that, so I started to help them.

Marie gently grabbed my arm. "They can do it. Just watch."

Sure enough, Al Jr was handing them the bread and a container of pimento cheese. "You're gonna love this stuff. Grandma Ethel makes it from scratch, and it is amazing! We got chips, apples, and Moon Pies for dessert! Milk or water for all to drink! If you need it, Lisa can help you pour it."

Holy cow! My kids were fixing their own lunch. Where'd they learn that? I was confused but proud.

After lunch, Ethel commanded the children to find a bed and read books to each other. "Anyone seven-to-fourteen-years-old is a reader."

Caroline piped in, "And I have an extra present for the ones who take a nap."

Amazingly, they all pranced into the bedrooms at the back of the house and shut the doors behind them.

Another miracle. My sisters and nieces were really good at herding cats.

The rest of the afternoon, we all contributed to the work that needed to be done. On Caroline's list was decorating the house, finishing present wrapping, pulling out the Christmas tree decorations, and prepping for Christmas Eve dinner. As we worked, we talked. We relived our Hazel damage and repairs. We talked about children, husbands, how partners could irritate, and what was great about them.

As we moved to other rooms in different groups, we got reacquainted. While Francie was helping Ethel with the table setting, Sue and I wrapped presents that had been hidden in a trunk.

I wanted to know more about the change that Sue had declared. "Sue, I need to understand your coming out as a gay woman. I didn't know a person could change like that almost overnight."

Without hesitation, Sue replied, "That's just it, Annie. I didn't change. I have been hiding who I am for a very long time. I never felt right as a girl who liked boys. Since I started helping with the business, I began to feel more powerful and smart. Momma stopped telling me what to wear, who to pick as friends, and pushing me to be like all the other girls. I don't think she realized she was doing it. She was just letting me be who I am. She saw me capable to run the business when she was away. Larry saw what was happening even before I did. Two years ago, I introduced him to Francie as my best friend. He got us to talk about what we like to do together and our dreams for the future. That was the first time I had ever said things out loud about what I really needed.

"In the spring, just before Momma came back from visiting Caroline for a week, Dad said he wanted me to tell Momma how I was feeling. I was terrified. I knew she wanted things normal and traditional. And I didn't want to make a tear in the family. Dad said, 'I have a story to tell you about your momma and this family. Ethel's second man and first husband, George Fox, was like God to her. In her mind, he did everything right after Frank did everything wrong. He was loyal, handy, steadfast, took on any problem and solved it with her. And he was the best father. When he married Ethel, he took on her three-year-old child, Marie, and loved her like his own. George supported your momma, Sue, when she was sick as if she was his blood relative. It was his idea to adopt you. Ethel said he believed every child should have a family.'

"Annie, Larry stopped as if to think how to say the next part. He said, 'Sue, I was none of those things. I tried to be. I tried to compete with the ghost of George, but I wasn't him. I also wasn't Frank. I would never leave her, even if she wouldn't marry me. Sue, who you think I am?'

"Annie, I had to think long and hard about this. I never thought about who Larry Dad was other than himself. Then I began to tick off the list in my head.

"I will never forget what I told him. I don't think I have even told Momma. Only Marie knows all this. I said to him, 'You are my dad. You love me all the way through my skin, into my brain, and my heart. You have business smarts. You are good at figuring out things. And you don't wait to see who will take care of something. You just do it. And then teach me how you did it. You are a clever man. A kind man. Momma is not the easiest person to get along with, but you help her find her goodness. You remind her what kind of person she really is—funny, hardworking, generous, loving, and the best sister. And you can take a penny and make it a dime any day.'

"Then, Annie, that big bear of a man stood up and gave me a hug. A giant bear hug, lifting me off the ground. He planted a kiss on my cheek and said, 'Do you want me to be anything else? Anybody else?'

"I finally got it. 'No, daddy, nothing else but you.'

"He said, 'Suzy, you need to be nothing else but you. Stop trying hard to be what you think others want. Can you do that?'

"Annie, I cried like a baby in his arms. When he lowered me to the ground, I ran out the door straight to the Francie's house. I told her everything. Then she summoned the courage to have that talk with her momma."

My heart was breaking for Sue. I can't imagine someone thinking they could not be who they were. That they couldn't think like they think, love who they love. I hugged her then stood to leave the room. "I'm going to find a job to do with Francie. I want to know her better. She must be terrific if you picked her."

I went to the kitchen and told my sister we needed to switch jobs. "I've tied so many bows on packages, my arthritis is kicking in. Besides, I want to spend some time with this cool kid."

Ethel pulled off her apron, handed it to me and said, "Here you go. Get the potatoes peeled for dinner. I have the turkey in the oven and just showed Francie how we make dressing in the Nash household. She's got that under control. Am I supposed to go do something in particular?"

I replied, "Nope. Just go make yourself useful. Sue's about finished with the wrapping."

She looked at me like she wanted to smack me. I giggled as she strutted out the kitchen door.

Francie was chopping onions and seemed to be tearing up. I hoped it was from the onions. She was not wearing an apron, so I pulled the one Ethel gave me over her head, turned her shoulders so I was in back of her, and tied the bow on the apron. "There we go. Making turkey dressing can be a messy job."

Grabbing a kitchen towel and tucking it into the belt of my dress, I went to the sink to wash the potatoes. At first, I wondered how to start a conversation with Francie. It really isn't like me not to be able to start a conversation.

I began like I would with anyone I just met. "Francie, tell me about yourself. Where did you grow up?"

"I'm an only child. My father is not around. He left us when I was six. Mother and I have lived lots of places. We always got settled when it was time for me to start school again. I guess I spent most of growing up time in Greensboro. The longest she worked anywhere was Cone Mills. We've lived in one of the villages there since I was fourteen. It was like a regular town with neighbors, schools, a church, and places for kids to play. All because they wanted the mill workers to stay put." Francie paused and looked at me like she had said something wrong.

To keep the discussion going I ignored her look. "I understand you were living in Burlington when you met Suzy. What took you there? How did you meet?"

I guess Francie felt safe. She went back to chopping and kept talking. "Mother didn't like the job at Cone Mills, so she went looking for a job at Burlington Mills. They hired her right away. I was bored and wanted to pull in some money. I found a job at a store that had a soda fountain. It was near the school so I could walk there after classes were out and stay until it closed. I worked every school day and on Saturday. Most days I worked the soda fountain, but sometimes they let me help the pharmacist mix up and bottle the medicine. I didn't have clothes to wear to a real job, but they gave me a uniform. With my first two paychecks I bought bobby socks and saddle oxfords. I liked my new look."

I was enamored with this person. She pulled me right into her story. I imagined her in new shoes and that white uniform with blue trim.

She was on a roll. "One Saturday Sue came to the soda counter and ordered a banana split. Evidently, I looked at her weird because she just stared at me. I asked her what kind of drink that was. Then she began telling me exactly how to make it. I said to her, 'Ice cream is the problem. We don't sell that here.'"

I laughed. I could totally hear Suzy giving instructions on the Ethel way to make a banana split. "There is a lot of experience making ice cream creations in our family. I guess you know that now."

Francie began to laugh. "Yeah, I know that now. And know all about washing laundry and folding clean clothes!"

Francie talked about learning to sew, having Suzy as a best friend, and hanging around the family as much as she could. It didn't take much prompting from me at all..

Then Francie made one comment that struck me that I didn't expect. "I just love Sue to pieces. I want to be with her always. But I know that is impossible. She needs a man to make a family."

I stopped peeling, dropped the knife, wiped my hands on the towel, and grabbed Francie by the shoulders. "Well, yes, technically that is true. To make a baby, she needs a man. If there is nothing else we fully understand in the Nash family, it's that a real loving family is made in many ways. I have no doubt Suzy wants a loving family no matter how is it made."

She leaned in and hugged me. I hugged her tight. Just like a Nash sister does. She laid her head on my shoulder and whispered, "Y'all are the nicest people in the whole wide world."

We pulled from the hug, and I smiled, "Naw. I don't know about that. We can be as mean as a starving cat. Just don't try to pull us apart."

I heard a vehicle pulling up next to the house. Peering out the window, I noticed it was getting dark outside sure enough. There was a truck full of men singing "Jingle Bells" at the top of their lungs. With the truck windows down, they probably could be heard all over Dix Hill. They obviously had not followed Ethel's command. Uh oh.

A huge Christmas tree was bending way off the end of the truck gate. It looked like asparagus that's way past its cooking time.

I grabbed Francie's hand and headed to the front door. We began singing in unison, "Jingle Bells. Jingle Bells. Jingle all the way."

Ethel, Sue, Marie with Emma Lou in her arms, and all the children came rushing to the front of the house bellowing the song. The Grand Nash Christmas had begun!

Behind the truck another car was tagging along. I didn't recognize the car, but there seemed to be a grown-up and child up front. I could make out that the back seat was full of wrapped boxes. The men climbed out of the truck and just stood watching as the car stopped. When the car lights turned off, a young boy wrapped in a big coat, mittens, and a toboggan got out of the passenger side and rushed around to the driver's side. The boy opened the door.

Ethel walked to my side, putting her hand in mine. She turned around to look at the front porch, "Marie, come here. I need you."

Marie was staring at the car. She did not move. The men stood like statues. The children stopped singing. I swallowed hard.

Ethel dropped my hand and took long steps to the driver's side of the car. She bent down to look at the driver, then leaned into the car. "Oh, sweet Jesus! Frank, is that you?"

She looked back at the boy saying, "Then you must be Eli." Softly she cupped her hand around the boy's cheek. "I'm so glad you came."

I was searching the car for other people. No one was there. Marie timidly walked toward the car.

We watched Frank struggle to get out of the driver's seat. I was not sure if it was because so many people were in the way, or if he really couldn't stand. No one had seen or heard directly from him since the accident. I wasn't sure about his condition. Evidently, he could drive. That was a good sign.

In my head I was trying to count the years. Eli must be eight years old. The same age as my Dianne. It looked like he was a much older child.

Caroline came through the front door and yelled to the group, "Christmas is coming y'all. Let's get that tree in the house! Frank, thank you for joining us."

At her command Larry, Al, Jon, and Joe began moving the tree from the truck. Obviously, Caroline put all this together. And the menfolk knew about it. I wanted to hug her so hard, but she was in army sergeant mode. Not a good time for affection.

When I looked back at the car, Ethel, Marie, Eli, and Frank were standing there in a group hug. Someone or everyone was sobbing. I cried out to whoever could hear, "Merry Christmas, one and all!"

Preparing the tree is the most celebrated activity

in our home. Our custom is that Jon did the decorating with the children. I would grab a cup of coffee, sit on the couch and watch father and children bond in a way that's like no other. Detangling lights would take patience. Stringing them round and round took creativity and planning. Jon was insistent they were spread just right. As the children unwrapped each ornament, they talked about its beauty and significance. This was always the best activity for father and child. I suggested we bring that tradition here.

Once the tree was up and stable, I called all the men into the room. "As a new Grand Nash Christmas ritual, the men will dress the tree with the children. We all brought a few ornaments to contribute to this tree. As each ornament is unwrapped, the children from each family can tell us about it before you men hang it up."

Frank asked Larry to go back to the car with him. They brought in three boxes. Eli recognized one and took it from his father's arms. Excitedly he said, "I packed this one. I know just what is in here. Can we go first?"

Standing at the living room door Ethel answered, "Of course you can, Eli. That would be the best way to start."

Frank took the other box from Larry and placed it on a table against the wall. Larry gave him his pocketknife to open it. Clearly it was store wrapped.

Marie helped him pull from the box the coolest present for the event. It was a record player in a wooden box labeled the *Pye Black Box*.

Marie yelled out, "Heavens to Betsy! Look at this.

I've seen this in magazines. She's a beauty!"

Al, the practical one, asked, "Hey, Frank, you got something to play on this?"

"I sure do, Al. Open that other box. I brought albums from my house."

Lisa, the oldest of my children, went running over. "Holy cow, it's Andy Williams, Frank Sinatra, and Bing Crosby! They are all here, Momma! Let's have a party!"

I answered back, "Well, let's get started. We need some music for our Christmas party."

The women grabbed a seat wherever they could find one. Francie and Sue brought in chairs from the kitchen table. The children sat around the naked tree. Caroline gently caressed the record player. She and Frank got it started with a recording from *White Christmas*. Since most of the adults had seen the movie, we sang along. It was the most beautiful moment. I could hardly keep from crying.

After the record stopped, I tapped Eli on the shoulder. "Okay, Eli, it's time for dressing the tree. You can start."

He nodded to his daddy to join him at the tree. As Eli stood next to Frank, I was struck by how much he looked like Frank back when I first met him. Even though he was Ethel's boyfriend, I thought he was so handsome. That child had Frank's dark hair and deep blue eyes. I looked over at Ethel. She must have noticed the same thing.

Leaning over to my ear, Ethel whispered, "Thank you, God, for giving him all of Frank's looks and none from his mother." We quietly giggled.

Eli pulled out a shiny blue round ornament and held it up for all to see. He said, "We have a lot like this one at home, all different colors. My favorite color is blue, so I brought this one. See the white paint on it? It looks like snow."

Eli grinned and stood proud when there were oohs and aahs from the children. He gave it to his daddy and said, "Put it way up high, so we can all see it."

Next, he unwrapped a crocheted white snowflake. He held it up and said, "Momma made this one. She sprayed starch on it to make it real stiff. It hangs better that way."

More oohs and aahs erupted. But Marie's Mary spoke through the admiration. "You have a momma? Why isn't she here?"

There was a momentary silence. Each child seemed to be looking at Frank. But Eli had the answer. "Momma doesn't like to ride a long way. She gets sick. She stayed home. We had Christmas there before we left. I got a Red Ryder BB gun."

Giggles and oohs broke the awkward quiet. Parents got the I-want-one-too look from their sons.

Eli finished with his last ornament. A hand-carved, wooden candy cane painted white and red. "Last year Daddy and I made this together. It's hard to make a curved shaped, but we did it."

I asked my family to go next. Lisa, then Jon Jr, then Dianne displayed their treasured ornaments. Each child brought two. Admiration was voiced all around.

After Marie's children proudly showed off the ornaments each brought, Al spoke to the group. He pointed to Marie holding Emma Lou.

Looking pleased with himself, and a little tipsy, Al said, "And here's my Christmas prize. Emma Lou is this year's Christmas star. And her momma's pretty special too."

Ethel stood and pushed her way through the crowd, "Oh good grief, Al. No more for you."

She was holding our mother's ragged but still stunning handmade angel. I gasped. Caroline did too. We had not seen it since the Nash sisters moved away from home.

Ethel walked to the front of the decorated tree. She hesitated and turned to us. "Children and grown-ups, this is the Nash family angel. It was made by a man and his wife who worked for Momma and Papa at the farm. This angel is over forty-five years old. She's had a little work done over the years, but mostly she has been in a box since 1931. Her body was carved from a branch off one of the walnut trees at our home place."

Ethel stroked the fragile angel as she spoke of each piece of her. "Momma made her white dress and sparkly belt. Her black hair was originally made from the fur of a farm animal. Her halo was made by twisting and braiding golden thread. As a child, I remember her being the prettiest thing on the tree. Now she is tattered and torn. Children, you probably know the story of *The Velveteen Rabbit*. This angel is kinda like that. She's been loved so much for so many years that she lost some of her loveliness. She's been in a box for a long time, like the rabbit. Now she needs to come out to be part of every Christmas for years to come. Since I doubt we are all going to be together like this again, I decided we should carefully pass her around to each family at Christmas. She will be cared for and loved by all y'all from now until the next children, grandchildren, and great-grandchildren come along."

Larry went to Ethel's side. He took the angel and placed it on the top of the tree. The children clapped. The mothers cried.

Caroline slipped from the room toward the kitchen. I noticed she lifted her apron and pressed it to her face. I followed her, but Sue beat me to her. I could not hear what they were saying, but they surrendered to the emotion of it all. Sue led Caroline to a chair and kneeled beside her. As I entered the kitchen, Sue's head was in her Auntie Caroline's lap. Caroline placed her hands on Sue's hair. They were both sobbing. It broke my heart. Was it happiness or sadness?

I leaned against the kitchen door, holding it shut. They needed this moment of privacy. I was lucky enough to be an observer, if not a participant.

Sue finally looked up at Caroline and said what we all were feeling. "Caroline, thank you for making all this happen. Especially for me. As I look at each one in that room, I feel blessed to have so many people I want to know better. I have not taken the time to know all the people in that room. That guilt is overwhelming."

Caroline cupped her hands around Sue's face. "Oh, dear Suzy. I mean Sue." Caroline chuckled a bit. "You are going to have to be patient with me. I've known you as Suzy for twenty-four years. I hope it doesn't take twenty-four more to get used to Sue."

Just as I knew she would, Sue said, "It's okay, Aunt Caroline. It's also taking me a while to get used to the new me."

Caroline placed her hands on Sue's arms and lifted her to her feet. Smiling at Sue, Caroline explained, "I also feel guilt, Sue. And anger. I'm mad that we have waited all my thirty-eight years to be together so fully. So intimately. I know my sisters as well as I can considering I have spent most of my life in an asylum. That knowing came from Annie and Ethel continuously caring for me. This summer has been the first time that I became a caregiver for them. I have felt guilty about always being the taker and never the giver. Today has been a day of recognition. Not of others for me. But me for myself. I am entirely covered with happiness. I never knew there was this kind of exhilaration in helping and doing for others."

I felt someone push hard on the door I was leaning against. I figured it was the elder sister who knew how to break things up. I gave a questioning look at Caroline.

She nodded. "I guess we can't hog the kitchen all night. Let my oldest sister in."

Sue backed away from Caroline and went to busy herself at the sink.

Dinner for eighteen was served at six thirty by Ethel, Caroline, and me—the Nash sisters. We piled plates full of food born of old family recipes and prepared in this kitchen by someone from each family. Since seating was a challenge, we handed filled plates for all to eat in their laps wherever they could find a place. Jon acted as the bartender. Ethel had commanded there'd be no alcohol with the meal. But the drinks from Jon were pretty special. He made sure everyone had Pepsi in wine glasses that he had brought from DC to use for our celebration. My children were especially excited because this would never happen at home.

The children sat in a circle on the living room floor except for the youngest ones. Jimmy sat on his daddy's lap eating off Al's plate anything that was safe for a two-year-old. In the back corner of the living room, there was an old upholstered chair. It reminded me of our thinking chairs. Marie was sitting quietly feeding Emma Lou. Madonna and child staring into each other's eyes.

Adults grouped themselves where conversations could continue. I noticed the men sat together at the kitchen table. Maybe it was to be near the food, but I really believe they too wanted to get to know each other better.

I walked over to the record player and searched the record collection for just the right music. Frank had brought a diverse selection. I shuffled through them a few times and then stumbled on the one I wanted. Some may think it odd, but I knew it was perfect. On the blue cover there was a picture of Leonard Warren. I knew his story. He was born to Russian Jewish immigrants and became famous not only as an opera singer but also for his baritone voice. He had studied in Italy. I was impressed that this was in Frank's collection.

I put the album on the player and turned the volume up so it could be heard in every room. I lifted the arm to set the needle just right. "America, the Beautiful" thundered from the Pye Black Box. I stood there watching the crowd listen intently.

After it was finished, Joe stood tall and proud and said, "Goooodness, that song gets me every time."

Jon responded, not only to Joe, "Me too, man! Although I never fought in combat, we sang it in many a bar during the war."

Somberly Joe raised his glass of Pepsi. "Jon, so did I. We sang whether drunk or sober all over Europe during the war. Play it again, Annie!"

I did. Three more times.

Ethel stepped over to me and summoned Caroline. "You guys may not know that this song is also a Nash sisters hit. You'd be surprised how often we sing this. It's definitely our stress reliever. Come on, girls, and let's sing it like we did in 1932!"

She continued telling the story. "Actually, I wrote the version we sang that day. Picture this: Our momma had died. Treasured possessions from home were loaded in Annie's car and in a horse-drawn wagon for Dianne and her Joe. The sisters were moving to a new place. Caroline was the first sister to move away. Annie was searching for happiness in the big city of Washington, DC. Dianne and Joe were moving to Burlington for good paying work. I hadn't decided where I was going to live. It was the beginning of new adventures for all of us, but sad too. I belted out this version as my sisters pulled away from my life."

Ethel sang loud and strong:

How beautiful the Nash girls are,
With family waves of love,
For moving away from memories
To new ones that we'll love!
Nash girls! Oh, Nash girls!
Let's shed our grace on thee
And crown ourselves with sisterhood
From Washington to Raleigh!

On the second time around, I squeezed Ethel's waist and sang with her. Caroline wasn't there on that day in 1932, but we've sung this enough since then she couldn't resist. Marie and Sue joined in. You can't be a Nash woman and not know this version.

When we finished the second time around, I suggested we all sing. "Okay, people, now that you have heard our singing ability, let's all sing the real version that was put to music by Samuel Bates in 1910."

Ethel held up the album cover saying, "And so magnificently sung by Leonard Warren tonight!"

And we did. The men, the women, and even the children tried to sing along. It was remarkable!

Most of the family was either laughing or wiping tears from their eyes. Laughing at our singing ability or feeling the emotion that song brought to us all.

After things settled down, the men went out on the back porch. Caroline was no longer worried about her checklist. She turned to the group and changed the plans. "All right. If the men aren't gonna help clean right now, we womenfolk aren't gonna either. Kids, you guys head back to the bedrooms. The one painted yellow is for the girls. That's where the cribs are set up for Emma Lou and Jimmy. Boys, you head for the bedroom with the cowboy wallpaper. Settle down in there. Santa is coming tonight, so you don't want to be up too late. He might just fly right by this house."

The children scrambled to one of the two bedrooms like cats heading to the food bowl.

I called out to the females in the family, "Y'all find a seat in the living room. I have something for you.

I headed to the kitchen to get one of the presents I brought for the ladies of the house. I fumbled around in the kitchen and finally rejoined the Nash ladies' group.

"Whew! It worked!" Marie said as she plopped on the sofa. She evidently had been successful putting down Emma Lou and Jimmy for the night. I brought out an open box and asked everyone to take one. Each reached in and pulled out a crystal wine glass. The oohs and aahs started again.

"Jon brought these back from eastern Europe for us to use for large formal gatherings. There can be no better time to use them and give each of you one as a remembrance of this Christmas."

Ethel spoke in a surprising not-so-Ethel way. "Annie, these are the magnificent! It is so generous of you and Jon to give them away!" Then in the totally Ethel way continued, "But I want two. Me and Larry both need to drink like we're in Europe."

Everyone laughed. Partly because she was funny,

but mostly because we were relieved it was really Ethel talking.

"Well, you are in luck, sister! We have a dozen! Pass the second box around, Ethel. I'm going to find something to put in this magnificence."

I went back to the kitchen and brought out six bottles of wine. Even more enthusiastic oohs and aahs erupted.

You would never think we had more to talk about since we'd been talking all day, but the opposite was true. There is never enough time for conversations while waiting. Waiting for Santa this time.

Caroline looked at her watch and signaled to me. It was ten o'clock before we knew it. Caroline morphed back into the organizer.

"The children are asleep in the bedrooms, and Suzy, Francie, and I are staying here to watch over them. You have one hour to clean up and arrange gifts for the children by the tree. Then gather yourselves up and retreat to your hotel. I am hitting the sack at eleven sharp."

Nearly as quickly as the children had scattered to their assigned bedrooms, the women folk did as they were told. Marie went to the porch and gave the men their orders. They unloaded boxes from the car and quietly planted the wrapped presents under the tree.

The sweetest thing happened next. Caroline brought in a bag full of crocheted stockings. One for each child with their name on it. She draped each over a chair or table.

"Well, lookie here, baby sister! You did learn to

crochet granny squares, and you put that talent to good use. These are incredible!"

She grinned. "Yeah, they turned out okay. I had fun doing them. And each child can take theirs home for Christmas at their house. Merry Christmas, everyone!"

At 10:50 five cars pulled away from the house leaving Francie, Sue, Caroline, and Joe alone with eight sleeping children.

CHAPTER 18 — CHRISTMAS DAY 1954

Marie
Having Ourselves a Merry Little Christmas

IT WAS AS COLD THIS Christmas morning as it was hot on the day Emma Lou was born. Breaking records on both ends of the thermometer. The group that came back to the hotel last night discussed the morning schedule. All feet would be on deck ready to go to The Hill no later than seven thirty.

By the next morning, I could wait no longer to get to my baby girl. I was awake at six and tried to stay still for another hour. At six thirty I tapped Al on the shoulder. "Good morning, Albert." I knew calling him that would wake him.

Planting a kiss on his cheek, I told him my agenda. "I am heading out. I'm about to explode. My body needs to get to my baby girl. And I need to help Caroline with the morning activities. You can stay here and catch a ride with someone."

Al pursed his lips and sent me an air kiss. "All right, baby. See you soon."

I went downstairs to grab a cup of coffee before leaving. Frank was sitting in the café with a steaming cup in his hand. "Good morning, Marie. You and I had the same idea. Sleep is not always necessary."

"Geez, I'd really love more sleep, but I have to get to Emma Lou. She needs me. Well, actually, I need her. I'm driving over to the house now. You wanna come, Daddy-O?"

"Yes, I do. But let me drive. I'll need my car there. We can't stay too late."

I was curious about so many things. A ride in the car is always a good time to talk. "That's a great idea. That'll give us more time to catch up. I'll leave our keys and a note for Al with the hotel manager. Be right back."

The drive time would not be enough time, but it got me started. "Why didn't Elizabeth come? I spoke with her on the phone about all the plans. She seemed excited about it."

It didn't seem like he wanted to talk about that. "You heard Eli. She doesn't like to ride too far."

Unexpectedly my blood pressure sharply rose. "Does she not like me? At least what I represent? For heaven's sake, I am a 26-year-old problem! It's time to get over being mad. She has an excuse whenever there is an opportunity to visit."

Luckily, we were sitting at a red light. Frank turned to me and gave me a sorrowful look. "It's not you, Marie. She is an angry person. She is struggling with mental issues and the blame for all that is me. There's no trust. No openness to this part of my family. I caught her talking to Eli about illegitimacy. I heard the words, 'Your daddy was a sinner before you—his legitimate child.' I burst in the room and started yelling. I nearly hit her. Eli jumped in front of me to protect his mother. My child needed to protect his mother against his father. How awful is that?"

The light turned green, but he did not move the car. He leaned his head on the steering wheel. I flashed back to that day of the wreck. His head was placed just like that.

"Oh, dear God! How could she be so merciless about a child? Even the meanest people in my young life never called me illegitimate. I worried about it until I became older and knew I could take anyone who wanted to say it. Frank, I don't know how you held back from striking her, but I'm glad you did. Did you talk to Eli about it later?"

Frank raised his head and looked straight ahead. "We haven't talked about it really. On the trip down, Eli said to me, 'Daddy, I'm sorry Mother was mean to you.' I pulled off the road. I told him that his mother was not mean, she was just sick."

"Poor Eli. He is such a brave boy. He has fit right in with his cousins. That's all Momma and I wanted. To know him and show him our love."

Taking a deep breath and straightening himself in the seat, Frank said something that broke my heart. "All I've ever wanted was forgiveness. From Ethel, you, my parents. And I married someone from whom I search for forgiveness. How crazy is that?"

We were sitting through a second green light. The

driver in the car behind us sat on his horn. I shot him the bird. "Let's pull over up there. I have one more thing to say."

Frank pulled the car off the road. He pushed the stick shift into park. I reached over and clasped my arms around his shoulders "Listen to me, Daddy. You are my first dad. You are me and I am you. There is no getting around that. No forgiveness is needed. If you and Momma hadn't loved each other, I would not be here. I would not have found Al and there would be no Al Jr, Mary, Jimmy, and Emma Lou. How could this world go on without them? Without us?"

I saw a tear fall from his eye. It made me tear up too. Momma and I can never resist the contagion of sadness. "Daddy, do you know why I was named Marie?"

He looked over at me and stroked my hair as he does so often. "No, I don't think so."

"Momma told my grandma right after I was born that she chose Marie because it meant wished for child. I have always felt wished for. Always felt loved. There is nothing illegitimate in that."

We sat for a few more minutes. Then in silence we drove to the Christmas house with me holding my daddy's arm.

When we arrived, there was quiet bustling around in the living room and the kitchen. Momma looked at me, then at Frank. "You two all right?" We both nodded.

Frank said, "Better than ever, E."

As he put his arm around Momma, I rushed to the bedroom to nourish my baby.

Caroline followed me to the bedroom to give me an update on all things here. "She slept all night. I was a bit nervous, so I woke her at five and gave her the bottle you left. In fact, all the children slept hard. Francie, me, and Sue stayed up talking till midnight, then crashed in the third bedroom with two double beds. Did you know Sue has a snoring problem? She sounds just like Ethel. It took me a bit to fall asleep, so I took my rock-a-bye baby pill. I heard nothing else until early this morning."

I crept into the bedroom as quietly as I could. I said to myself, "No one was stirring. Not even a mouse." I picked up my little girl, grabbed a diaper, and slipped back to the living room thinking chair. This was perfect. I had a lot to think about.

Sue pulled up a chair beside me and sat down. "Marie, I never took the time to thank you for my birthday present. At first, I was confused by it. A compass? What will I use it for? Am I going on a trip and need to know the direction I am going? I did some research. That's what my teachers used to tell us to do. I went to the library in Burlington. They have a good set of encyclopedias, and I looked it up. What could it mean? Especially for me? You may already know this, but the word compass is *com*, meaning together, and *passus*, meaning pace or step. It could lead me on a safe journey. The book said it also represents balance. I need balance in my life. Sometimes I feel lost in who I am and what I am supposed to be. The compass can also bring me hope that I can find my way. I think family is my balance. Without y'all I would be wandering around trying to get where I should be. Marie, it is the loveliest gift. I keep it with me every day."

Sue pulled it out of the pocket of her skirt. I admired it as I did when I first saw it. It was perfect for Sue. She leaned over and kissed my cheek. Then she leaned in farther and kissed Emma Lou on her head. "Emma Lou, you have the greatest person for a mom."

I took my free arm and wrapped it around Sue's shoulder. "I'm glad you see the importance in the compass. We all need what it symbolizes."

Our sweet moment was interrupted by the sound of children moving around in their bedrooms. Caroline walked across the living room down the hall in their direction. I could hear her tell them the rules. "Good Christmas morning, children. You can get up and go to the bathroom. But you can't come into the living room until everyone is ready. I'll let you know when."

I could hear my Al Jr asking if Santa had found us.

Carolina replied, "I can report that Santa did indeed leave something for each of you. But you can't come out here until all your parents are here."

Within a few minutes, which probably seemed like forever to the children, Ethel went down the hall to the bedrooms and called to the children. "Okay, everybody, come here this minute! There are so many packages making a mess in the living room. Somebody needs to find their rightful owners!"

The stampede to the living room began. Annie spoke up in her sophisticated way, "Orderly, children! Orderly! We start with what Santa brought. Your mom or dad has that with them, so enjoy that as a family."

For the next half hour, there was a delirious and cheerful scramble of Nash people.

The air smelled like country ham, cinnamon buns, and hot coffee. My favorite smells in the world. I walked to the kitchen to help with breakfast. Larry and Frank were in there cooking eggs and watching over the biscuits baking. There was chatter. Men conversing like they always do. Talking sports, how to repair things, and the weather. Nothing changed in their conversation when I entered the room.

Larry welcomed me with no expectations to take over the cooking. "Merry Christmas, little girl! Do you want a cup of coffee? I can't let you dive into the cinnamon rolls yet. You know how your momma is about routine."

With a knowing grin on his face, Frank answered, "I know what you're talking about, Larry. I was hoping you had fixed her by now."

Larry laughed at the impossible. "Hell, Frank. There ain't no fixin' Ethel. You just have to get out of her way. You know that better than me."

I looked at them both. "This is the best, my two dads!" Neither probably knew I wasn't talking about the food.

After all the presents were given to the appropriate persons, everyone could settle back and start opening. Al Jr, the youngest in the group that could understand what needed to happen, shouted to the group, "At my house we open gifts one person at a time, and we all watch."

Rather than oohs and aahs, there were less pleasant sounds coming from the crowd.

Then Momma spoke up. "Little Al, you are right. That is the way we should do it. To be respectful of each gift given. But there are nearly twenty people to wait for. It will be dark before we get through it. So open with your family and before the day is over, go say thank you to the person who gave you each gift."

Caroline went to the record player and put on an album of music we all knew. As the present opening was happening, we listened.

Dashing through the snow
In a one-horse open sleigh,
O'er the fields we go,
Laughing all the way.

At the chorus we all joined in. We knew those words so well.

Jiggle Bells,
Jingle bells,
Jingle all the way.
Oh, what fun it is to ride in a one-horse
open sleigh, hey!
Jiggle Bells,
Jingle bells,
Jingle all the way.

Breakfast was consumed. Children quieted. And adults began cleaning up from the festivities.

Annie came over and whispered in my ear. "The surprise guests are coming."

I looked out the front window and sure enough, about a dozen people were heading to the house. I called Caroline over to greet them with us. We stepped on the porch together.

In front of us there was a crowd that represented our history as sisters. Even though I knew this was going to happen, I could not hold back the tears.

First in the group was a tall man whose back was a bit bent, and he walked with the help of a cane. Caroline yelled out, "Dr. Tom! I am so glad you could come to meet all my family!"

The others held back as Dr. Redmond, Caroline's doctor for over fifteen years, came forward with hand extended for a very doctor-like handshake with Ethel, Annie, and Caroline. "I am glad to see you all. Merry Christmas. He moved over to me taking my hand. "It looks like you have healed well. I am glad to see that."

I replied nearly as formal as he was. "Dr. Redmond, I probably don't know all the things you have done for me and Caroline this year. But I want you to meet the product of your goodness."

I turned back to the house and called for Al to bring Emma Lou. "And get Frank to come out also."

Frank stepped out holding Eli's hand. "Eli, this is Dr. Redmond. He helped me heal from the accident. He is one of the people to whom I owe my life."

Dr. Redmond seemed happy to see them. "Well, I'll be. There is the miracle man. Eli, do you know your dad is a miracle? He might just be the strongest, hardworking, positive man I've ever known. I know you must be proud of him."

Eli responded with a big smile. "Yes, my dad almost died. Thank you for helping him get well for me."

"Child, I think your dad worked hard to get well because he had you to be well for."

Caroline interrupted with an excited shout. "Belle, oh dear Belle, is that you?"

Ethel, Annie, and Caroline ran to Belle and enveloped her in a giant group hug. Seeing this, there was not a dry eye on the porch.

As they pulled from the hug, Belle said with a lot of love, "It's me, sweet woman. I haven't seen you in so long, I was not going to let this chance get by. Joe told me there was a Christmas party going on. And you know how I like parties. Look who else wanted to see you!"

Up walked a family of four. The man looked very much like Belle. As I understood who they were, my heart was breaking for Caroline. I had never met this family but knew so much about them from her.

With hesitation, Caroline walked to the family and nervously spoke. "Mr. Parker. Mrs. Parker. It is so lovely to see you. Thank you for coming."

As Caroline reached out her hand to them, out stepped a tall, smiling boy and a young girl. Both of them ran up to Caroline and grabbed her up in a hug. Evidently it was a bond that knew no time. They were children full of love for a woman who had made a scary mistake with them. The bond erased that mistake. And Caroline felt it.

She looked at the Parkers and said, "I am sorry. I will always be sorry if I did anything to hurt these dear people."

Mrs. Parker shook her head and said, "Caroline, look at these wonderful, growing children. You had a part in how great Ida and Billy are. No forgiveness necessary."

I caught Frank's eye and grinned.

Ida looked a bit confused by the forgiveness discussion. "Caroline, can you help me with my studies? Mom says I need a tutor. I think you would be perfect."

Now Caroline was confused.

Then Billy spoke, "I miss you, Caroline. I remember you from when I was a preschooler. You were always so good to me. And fun."

Caroline looked back at Ethel and me. Her eyebrows raised. Her head moved back straight over her shoulders. The smile was wide and proud.

She spoke to the Parkers, "I'd really like to see more of y'all. I need good people in my life. My family lives all over the place. I don't get to see them much."

Belle came to add her contribution. "Caroline, we all need good people. There's never enough to go around."

As goodbyes were being said to our visitors, someone in the house had started up the record player and turned the volume way up.

Oh beautiful for spacious skies for amber waves of grain . . .

I walked back into the house. Sue, Momma, Aunt Caroline, and Aunt Annie found me. Arm in arm we stood. Absorbing the last two days.

Family began moving inside. Picking up the remains of a Grand Nash Christmas. Packing for their trip home.

Daylight joy and happiness was turning into evening sadness. I knew what it meant. We would be leaving one another, going our separate ways. I will miss the proximity to each of them. I will never forget what we experienced here this weekend. The luxury of talking whenever we wanted to about anything that came to mind. Listening when someone needed to be heard. Witnessing my family as mothers, sisters, aunts, uncles, husbands, fathers, and partners. Cousins growing up knowing each other. And most of all, touching an arm or holding a hand whenever we needed one another. We can't replicate these two days. Never have. Never will. But we can have more times, but different, together. We just have to make it happen somehow.

Trying to hold back the tears, I circled my arms around these Nash women and pleaded, "Let's not forget this. Not only this weekend, but this whole year. Okay? We've all come through a lotta change. I am proud of us."

Annie said it best, "We will not forget. We can't. We are changed individuals. A better us in so many ways." She stood tall and held her hand over her heart. "These two days reminded me how we can be. A larger, stronger, loving family."

I think each of us felt something special in these last moments of the Grand Nash Christmas weekend. Then pragmatic Ethel brought us back to the leave-taking moment and moved us on. "Okay. Let's talk next week. I will set aside a night a week for each of you."

Caroline shouted, "I want Monday."

I said, "Sundays are my night."

Annie said, "I want Wednesday evening and Saturday morning."

Sue said, "We live together, so I get you anytime I want. But when you move away, I want Thursday."

And there it was in action. Setting the new plan. The Nash family. Bonded forever.

A Message to My Readers

Dear Readers,

I write for my enjoyment. I rewrite to pull you into the story and enrich the characters. My editor polishes it off so you, when you close the last page, will want more.

The only way I know if all this works is through feedback from you and recommendation of the books to others.

Would you please take a few minutes to rate and write a review of this book on Amazon.com, Goodreads.com, or the bookstore websites wherever you purchased the book? My characters and I would be so appreciative.

Gratefully yours and until next time,
Leatha Marie

leathamarie.com
leathamarie.authorsites.co/

ABOUT THE AUTHOR

LEATHA MARIE'S CAREER HAS concentrated on the development and nurturing of children and those adults who teach. She taught public school in rural North Carolina where she learned the difference between street smarts and book smarts—and the value of both. The majority of her experience has been in mentoring the next leaders in early childhood education corporations. All the while, she has gathered stories of life, loyalty, challenge, and how resilience leads to success. Lately, her work has included coaching, writing, and training business managers to become more leader than boss. Reading non-fiction books and articles has fed Leatha's talents. Reading fiction for pleasure has fed her soul. Her first novel in the The Nash Sisters series was published in 2019. *My Turn* is the third novel in the series. The fourth is in early stages!

Made in the USA
Columbia, SC
17 May 2022

60536583R00131